The Resistance

Even the book morphs!
Flip the pages
and check it out!

Look for other **ANIMORPHS**®
titles by K.A. Applegate:

the andalite chronicles

The Resistance

K.A. Applegate

AN
APPLE
PAPERBACK

SCHOLASTIC INC.
New York Toronto London Auckland Sydney
Mexico City New Delhi Hong Kong

Cover illustration by David B. Mattingly
Art Direction/Design by Karen Hudson/Ursula Albano

ISBN 0-439-11521-3

12 11 10 9 8 7 6 5 4 3 2 1   0 1 2 3 4 5/0

Printed in the U.S.A.
First Scholastic printing, November 2000

The author wishes to thank Ellen Geroux for her help in preparing this manuscript.

For Michael and Jake

The Resistance

CHAPTER 1

My name is Jake.

But you already know who I am.

Not "Commander Jake" or "Chief Jake" or even "Captain Jake." Just Jake. That's what everyone calls me, even now.

Now that my entire life is devoted to strategy and preparation and battle against the Yeerks.

It's my job to keep us alive. It's my job to think about the moral and practical consequences of our actions.

I like to think I'm not one of those guys with a huge ego. But sometimes I feel like no one notices what I'm doing. And it bothers me. Both that no one notices *and* that I care.

Okay, I get "Prince Jake," but only from Ax. Definitely not at home.

"Jake!" My mom. "Thank goodness you're home. It's about to storm and I'm late to pick up Homer from the vet. Where have you been?"

Mom doesn't have a clue about the Yeerks. I'd like to keep it that way.

"Out," I said. Exhaustion can make you act like a jerk.

Truth is, it's been months since I slept a full night. There's no time for sound sleep anymore. Rachel, Cassie, and I barely make it to school these days. Marco and Tobias don't make it at all.

Because the Yeerks are on the move. Big time.

Ax monitors the Yeerks' Z-space transmissions day and night. Most of the important stuff is too carefully encrypted for even Ax to decode using cobbled-together, human-made components. But little pieces of casual conversation point to one thing. Something major. Something huge.

As if we needed Z-space eavesdropping to tell us what was already abundantly clear.

The end is near.

We don't know when or how it will come. But we know it's coming.

When the Yeerks attacked a U.S. aircraft carrier not long ago, they took a huge and semi-public step toward all-out, full-scale invasion.

We managed to hurt the effort enough to make the Yeerks retreat. But they definitely haven't given up.

"Listen carefully." Mom grabbed her keys, put them in her purse. "It's going to start raining any minute. I want you to close all the windows in the house right away. Then I need you to clear out the storage room in the basement."

And I'd been hoping to catch five minutes on the couch. "Uh, Mom? Can't I do that tomorrow? Please?"

"Nope. The contractor's coming first thing in the morning to give an estimate on the new rec-room. Besides, it'll earn you twenty bucks."

Mom pulled on her rain jacket. "I piled some storage boxes at the top of the stairs. If you want a cozy place for you and your friends to hang out, I suggest you get to work."

Cozy place. I almost laughed out loud. There wasn't going to be a cozy place *anywhere* if we didn't come up with a plan to stop the Yeerk invasion.

I opened the door to the basement. A tall stack of cardboard boxes blocked my way. Fine. I was leader of a group of resistance fighters,

3

Earth's only hope for freedom, and I had to clean the basement to earn a lousy twenty bucks. Talk about irony.

I gave the boxes a gentle nudge. Not meaning for them to tumble to the bottom of the stairs. Which they did.

"Jake!" Mom frowned and paused at the door. "I'm counting on you." Then she was gone.

I began to close windows in the living room and kitchen. The sky was getting darker, heavy and threatening. Yeah, there was going to be a storm.

I'm not a poetic kind of guy. Usually. But this afternoon I couldn't help but notice that today's weather situation was a good metaphor for my mood.

I'd just come from an after-school meeting with the others. Rachel, Tobias, Cassie, Marco, and Ax. It was not a pleasant meeting. Tempers were blown. Time was running out and we still couldn't agree on anything.

Ever since Marco had to morph in front of his dad, there's been talk of dropping our cover all together. Tell people who we are. Tell the media who we are and what's really happening on Earth. So that we can all start fighting back. Well, those of us who aren't Controllers.

There is a definite plus to telling our secret. But there's a downside, too.

Rachel's dying to go public, kick butt, and never look back. Typical. Not that she's necessarily wrong, but she doesn't always think about consequences.

That's my job.

As I see it, the only reason the Yeerks haven't yet made a full-scale, totally out-in-the-open attack is because the stealthy approach is still working for them. It must be.

So if we blew the Yeerks' cover, what would be their incentive for not obliterating every major city in the world?

They could do it. We knew they weren't opposed to using human nuclear technology. But they wouldn't even need it. A couple of Blade ships could destroy a city, and the Yeerks would only lose a few million potential hosts in the process.

And we couldn't risk that.

But we had to do something . . .

Because the infestation has been going on for a long time now. There are maybe thousands of Controllers in my hometown alone. Too many people pass in and out of the Yeerk pool for us to keep careful track of the evidence.

Bottom line: Earth is losing its soul. People have to know. There's no doubt in my mind about that. They have to be made to see. But going public, taking that major step . . .

Sometimes, it's too much. The decisions, the pressure. The basement . . .

I went down to the basement. Past the running washing machine. On to the back room, dragging a stack of boxes, a marker, and a tape gun.

It was dark. A cotton pull cord brushed my arm and I yanked it. The single bulb that dangled at the center of the room brightened. The light made me squint and look away.

Stacks of boxes overflowing with papers. My old bike. A broken lamp. A whole roomful of junk.

I tripped over a pile of loose papers. Numbers, columns of figures, the words "Mutual Fund Allocation." I threw the papers in one of the empty boxes. Labeled it: MOM'S STUFF.

I grabbed another stack of papers off the floor. At the top of the first page a kid had scrawled: "What I Did This Summer." In the corner were the stamped words: GOOD JOB!

Tom's old schoolwork. From before he became a Controller. I threw the stack into another box and started to write his name on the lid. Stopped and crossed it out. Printed: TRASH. I didn't have a brother anymore.

That depressing fact made me think back to the afternoon's meeting.

Ax favored continued secrecy, at least until the Andalite fleet arrived.

No one really believes the Andalites are coming. Not even Ax. But hope, even false hope, is better than none at all.

Over my head, another shelf of junk.

HOLIDAY DECORATIONS went next to my mom's stuff. I reached above my head for the next box.

It was almost too big to manage. I heaved it to the floor. A Post-it note on top said, *For Jake from Grandpa G* in Mom's handwriting. So this was the box he'd left me in his will? Mom must have been saving it for my next birthday or something.

It was an old-fashioned chest covered in dark, moldy leather. Decorative tooling and metal trim made it look kind of fancy. The slightly curved lid displayed the name *Fitzhenry* in raised leather letters.

The name was familiar. Had I met some Fitzhenrys at a family reunion? Mom's cousins?

I reached to open the lid of the chest and the light went out.

The washing machine stopped.

I could hear the wind and the rain beating against the panes of the small basement windows, rattling them loudly.

CRAAASSSSHHHH!

I crept through darkness toward the source of the sound.

Just enough light seeped in from outside for

me to see the large, fallen tree branch that had smashed the glass in the basement window. Wind and rain funneled inside.

Another crisis.

It would be nice if they were all so small.

CHAPTER 2

I stumbled up the stairs, sneakers crunching broken glass. The rechargeable flashlight was in the kitchen, plugged in next to the stove. I grabbed it and the roll of duct tape from the kitchen drawer and ran back downstairs.

I placed a sheet of cardboard over the broken window and taped the edges to the wall. The basement was completely dark now except for the flashlight beam.

I went back to the antique chest. The raised leather tooling was thick with dust. I lifted the lid and aimed the flashlight inside.

Some sort of suit coat, folded and packed on top. Dark blue wool. A row of large brass buttons

9

nearly the size of quarters. I lifted it out of the box and set it, still folded, on the floor.

Beneath the coat was an assortment of small objects. Old medals attached to faded pieces of colored fabric. A long, corroded knife with two edges. At the base, where a handle should have been, there was a curved metal ring and two holes. Like the knife was meant to attach to something.

There wasn't much more in the box. A tin cup, a comb, a gross old toothbrush that looked handmade. I wondered which box to put this stuff in. The crumbling chest wasn't going to last much longer.

BANG! The back door, slamming shut.

"Mom?" I hollered. "Is that you? How's Homer?"

No answer. I left the contents of the box on the floor and carefully made my way upstairs. The storm seemed to be quieting.

"Mom," I called again. "The power went out and . . ."

I turned and saw him standing there, in the doorway between the kitchen and the living room. Looking at me. Silent.

"Whoa, man, you scared me," I said, trying not to sound as startled as I felt.

Tom. Not my brother anymore. A Yeerk. I pretended I didn't know that, pretended everything was normal. My family's survival depended on my acting skills.

"Some storm, huh?" I said.

I smiled. Tom didn't.

"If the power doesn't come back on, maybe we won't have school tomorrow."

"It'll be back on in a few minutes," Tom said flatly.

"Right. Hey, want to help me organize the basement? Lots of cool stuff down there."

The last thing I wanted was to hang around with Tom. He really freaked me out. He was brother and alien, sibling and enemy. I always worried I'd let something slip, something that would give everything away. But the nice younger brother act was essential.

"No," he said absently. "Tell Mom I won't be here for dinner. I have to be someplace."

"Where?"

He didn't answer. Just walked away.

"Preparations," he muttered, heading down the hall.

I tensed. His Yeerk was stressed. Talking to itself. I pretended I hadn't heard.

"Okay. Later."

Maybe he was just talking about school. Maybe I was the one cracking up.

I went back down to the basement. Propped the flashlight against a cabinet so that it shone

11

on the wall behind the old chest. Picked up the blue jacket with the big brass buttons.

THUNK!

Something slipped from between the folds and hit the floor.

I shook out the jacket, looking for more hidden objects. It was long. Just about my size in the shoulders, but reaching all the way down past my knees. With a tear in the left breast.

I refolded it, placed it into the box, and picked up the object that had fallen on the floor. It was a book. Leather cover. Pages that didn't quite align at the edges.

I crouched closer to the flashlight and opened the cover. The front leaf read, *Lieutenant Isaiah Fitzhenry*. I flipped to the first page.

We know General Forrest and his cavalry are out there . . .

Suddenly, I remembered where I'd heard the name Fitzhenry. He was the great-great-uncle Grandpa G had talked about. The Civil War hero.

And this had to be his journal.

All the stuff in the box made sense now. The coat was his uniform. And the knife.

I thumbed through the pages. The handwriting was neat and straight. Fancier than people write today. Some of the letters took a second to recognize, but on the whole the writing was pretty easy to read. Words were neatly crossed out in places. One entire page was smeared with ink and brown stains. I turned back to the first page.

"Jake?"

I heard Mom at the back door. Homer's claws skittering across the kitchen tiles.

Then, a straining whine from the laundry room. The washing machine laboring back to life. The bulb overhead flickered twice, then shone brightly.

"Jake?" Mom called again from the kitchen.

I set the diary on top of the blue wool uniform.

"Coming!" I called.

I turned away from the box. Stopped short and turned back. The old journal lay open.

We know that General Forrest and his cavalry are out there. But will he come? Will he ever come? And if he does, shall we be ready?

I paused, then closed the book and shut the lid of the box.

That was a different war.

A long time ago.

CHAPTER 3
Isaiah Fitzhenry

Sinkler's Ridge, Tennessee.
December 23, 1864.
Early morning.
We know General Forrest and his cavalry are out there. But will he come? Will he ever come? And if he does, shall we be ready?

When we went into camp two days ago, Major Charles Shaw held the command of our detachment. Major Shaw died last night, struck down not by Rebel fire, but by fever.

I, Lieutenant Isaiah Fitzhenry, command the detachment now. The mission is in my hands.

"Lieutenant!"

Sergeant Raines burst through the door and

strode toward me, boots crashing across the wood floor. His bootfalls sounded like the echo of artillery and I jumped to my feet with reflex action.

I pray that I, too, am not succumbing to fever.

"Have we received an answer?" I asked quickly.

I'd sent him to telegraph for new orders. Marching orders, I hoped. We had to move east, rejoin the regiment, get the sick men to safety.

"No, sir," Raines replied.

His anxious gaze shifted to the floor, then out the window, then back to the floor. His clenched jaw looked tight enough to break a tooth.

"What then?"

Raines's boots appeared at once wet and stiff. They were covered in mud, and frozen, no doubt. I glanced through the window of the tumbledown house we'd taken as headquarters. A vile mixture of rain and snow was falling outside.

I wiggled my own toes. Only the faintest sensation. And I know I am better off than most of the men.

Raines raised his piercing blue eyes.

"It's the telegraph line, sir," he said. "It's been cut."

I felt blood drain from my face.

We were cut off.

15

Raines shifted his weight.

"It's General Forrest's Confederate cavalry, Lieutenant. One of Forrest's men cut the line."

"How do you know?" I shot back. I prayed Raines was mistaken. "Can you be sure?"

"Our boys on picket duty caught the Reb that done it, and brought him into camp."

I looked back out the window. The mighty blue mist-shrouded mountains loomed like a silent approaching enemy. Sniffing us out, roping us in, preparing to strike.

So Forrest was near!

"Is the prisoner outside?"

"At the hospital tent, sir. He tried to escape and took a shot in the arm."

Sinkler's Ridge is a single street of drab clapboard and log buildings. A worth-nothing town that we never would have seen. If it weren't for the junction.

Two minor rail lines pass through here. Minor only in size, for they carry goods to General Sherman's army. Vital supplies like hardtack, coffee, coats, tents, rifles, shoes, socks, artillery, and ammunition.

Everything necessary to sustain the campaign.

If we lose the junction, the Rebels could destroy Sherman's army. Union victories at Vicksburg and Atlanta won't mean a thing.

"Keep the Sinkler's Ridge rail junction in Union hands."

Oh, how simple those orders sounded two days ago when the men stood tall and sixty strong.

One's circumstance can change so quickly.

My men are dropping like flies, the fever is spreading, and it is cold.

So cold.

Of the many things we need, I would settle for blankets.

"How many men are ready for service?" I asked.

"Fewer than twenty-five, Lieutenant. If Forrest comes this way with even a small force, we ain't going to be able to hold them and that's a fact."

Today is my twentieth birthday. Two years in the army now and by all accounts a man, yet I do not look it. Though tall, I'm thin. Though an officer, my hair falls across my forehead like a baby's curls and no amount of combing keeps it back.

The men must see me as more boy than man.

Respect is earned. I know such regard takes time.

But I feel I can prove my strength, show that my heart is free of fear and weakness, that I am built to serve the Union and prevail.

"If we can't telegraph for new orders, we must obey the orders we have."

"Lieutenant?" I could hear the shock in Raines's voice.

"Prepare to defend our position. If the Rebels want this junction, they have to fight for it and fight darn hard. Am I right, Raines?"

Raines was a good man, resilient and hard. I'd never seen defeat in his face and I didn't see it now.

"Yes, sir!"

"Assemble the men and reassign duties. But first, alert the hospital tent that I'll be by directly. I will see the prisoner."

"Yes, sir," Raines repeated, saluting as he turned on his noisy heels.

A tin whistle's jaunty tune filtered through the window. It was the town boy I'd seen before, and his friend with a drum. They marched back and forth on the main street, backs straight, heads high. Playing and drumming.

"When Johnny comes marching home again, hurrah! Hurrah! . . ."

They'd been practicing.

They were ready.

When we see action, I might have to call on them.

CHAPTER 4

The biting wind cuffed my ears as I walked toward the tents.

We'd set up at the end of the main street, just across the tracks from the depot. One large tent served as the hospital. A dozen dirty-white wedge tents formed two rows of flapping canvas shells. If the fever continues to spread, we won't need half the tents we've got.

I tucked my journal into my right pocket and crossed the tracks.

Ma sent the journal in her last package, in a box meant for Thanksgiving, but not received until just days ago. The chocolate and potatoes were still good, but the turkey was rotten and the cake had turned hard as mortar. I wish I had it now to add to munitions.

Other men kept journals, but never me. Why remember all the things I wanted to forget?

In her letter, Ma told me why.

"You'll be an old man someday, Isaiah. You'll think back on this war — on the boys you knew and the towns you saw — and you'll need to remember."

"Lieutenant!"

Sergeant Raines appeared from behind the hospital tent, his face contorted in alarm and confusion.

"There's some men coming into camp, sir." The intensity of his voice stopped my heart. Forrest?

"Who?" I yelled, falling into a run. "What approach?"

"Not sure, sir."

"For God's sake, Raines! Speak up."

"I guess they must be runaway slaves been hiding back up in the hills."

I started to breathe again, annoyed with Raines for getting so excited. For getting me so excited. We had no time for distractions. This would be a trivial matter, a corporal's job.

"What do they want?" I said shortly. "Food?"

"No, sir," Raines said weightily. "They say they've come to fight."

A laugh escaped me before I could stop it. A nervous mix of surprise and annoyance at a preposterous idea.

I rounded the back corner of the hospital tent and froze in my tracks.

Three dozen men, perhaps more, stood before me in an uneven line. Tall, short, wide, slight. Mismatched shirts and pants unified by a state of profound wear, as though each man had been born into the world with just one suit of clothes and was wearing it still.

Such blistering sores on feet I've never seen even on my own ill-provisioned men. Mere suggestions of boots. Near them on the dirt rested raggedy knapsacks tied to rickety sticks.

I looked at the faces last, at features as diverse as those in our detachment, at dark skin of varied hues.

"What'll we do?" Raines demanded, breaking the silence of my observation. "Use them as contrabands?"

Contraband was what we called these people early in the war, back before the Emancipation Proclamation. Back when the Union first realized that it could employ former slaves. Not as soldiers, but as laborers.

I didn't answer Raines, for there were more than thirty faces fixed on me, each wanting an answer.

Whom to address? Which face to look at? I met one tall man's eyes, but his gaze dropped instantly to the dirt.

So I moved toward the tattered wall of men and said, somewhat shakily, "I am Lieutenant Fitzhenry. I see you're here to help the Union cause. I am glad of that, for we need your help. A Rebel attack is imminent."

At this, a wave of whispers rustled through the men.

"We must prepare defenses. That is my sole concern," I continued. "There's no time to construct gabions or chevaux-de-frise. We need earthworks, simple and straightforward. And we need them dug fast."

A smallish man with a wide-brimmed hat stepped out of the line.

"We're here to fight, sir."

I ran my eyes up and down the line of men, pondering how to phrase my rejection in clearer terms.

"Do you understand that soldiering takes many forms? That fatigue work is as much a part of victory as . . ."

"We'll dig your defenses, Lieutenant. But when the attack comes, we want to fight."

"What's your name?" I said.

"It's Jacob."

"You will refer to me by my rank," I said sharply.

"Yes, Lieutenant."

"Surely you know you cannot fight," I said with rising frustration. "Surely you know it's impossible."

"We're free men, Lieutenant. Everyone in this line would rather die than lose that freedom."

Again, whispers ruffled the line, obvious support for Jacob's words.

"And I know your men are sick with fever," Jacob continued. "You need men, Lieutenant. Here we are."

"Fighting is out of the question!" I shot back, glancing at Raines. The presumption in Jacob's candor and logic disturbed me. "We can provide you with minimal provisions — boots, stockings, a bit of food — in exchange for labor. We need entrenchments dug! Raines will distribute shovels and pickaxes and whatever else he can find. Fatigue work is all I can offer you," I shouted, exasperated. "It's all I can offer!"

They couldn't fight. It was impossible. My own men would not stand for it. The townspeople, now only weakly pro-Unionist, would rebel. An armed force must be unified, not divided!

And the men were untrained. They could not shoot muskets if they had them.

Yet we were in desperate need of men. With just twenty-five, we were a handful against a multitude. What did Forrest's force number? Hundreds?

More?

"Follow me, all of you!" Raines yelled, marching off toward the supply shed.

Raines's order was premature.

Jacob hadn't accepted.

He stood still, staring at me with eyes dark as night.

"We'll do a job to make Lincoln proud," he said finally, smiling faintly. Reluctantly, he marched away after Raines. The other men fell in after him.

I feared I hadn't won the argument. Indeed, I felt it had only just begun.

CHAPTER 5
Jake

Brrrr-ing!

I snapped awake. Grabbed the phone before my eyes were open. Put it to my ear. Opened my eyes.

"Hello?"

"Oh, hi, Jake." Cassie.

I groaned. The clock said 4:55 A.M.

"Sorry. I must have hit the wrong speed dial. But while I have you, I've been meaning to tell you that Toby asked me to thank you for loaning her your history notes. I think she likes you."

"Great," I said. "Okay. Go feed the chickens or whatever you vet types do at this hour of the morning."

"Give the animals their meds, actually. 'Bye."

Cassie. Talking nonsense all so she could work in the code word "Toby." It meant one thing. There was trouble for the free Hork-Bajir.

I had to get to their valley. Now.

I crept from my room to the hall and listened. Not a sound. The house was chilly, the carpet cold under my bare feet. I neared Tom's room and carefully cracked open the door. A bulge of covers. He was asleep.

I watched for a minute. No movement. I walked into the room. The floor creaked loudly. I froze. Still, Tom didn't stir. I reached out and touched the covers, my heart beating in my ears. What would I say if he woke up?

I pressed gently. The covers rebounded softly. Pillows. The bed was stuffed with pillows.

Tom was out on Yeerk business.

Again.

Quickly, quietly, I made my way down the hall, past my parents' bedroom. Both were sleeping soundly.

I moved silently down the stairs. Slugged down a glass of orange juice from the container and wrote my parents a note.

Went running early. Going straight to school. Don't worry, I'll catch an Egg McMuffin.

I stuck the note to the coffeemaker and walked out the back door. Climbed the maple tree and in near darkness morphed a peregrine falcon. And in no time I rose high into the early-morning sky.

The predawn city spread beneath me. Every person on the street, in every car and every house, was suspect now. Anyone could be a Controller. And Controllers could be anywhere. But there were fewer of them in the woods. As the houses and roads became less frequent and farther apart, as the trees began to thicken, I began to breathe easier again.

I always think I know how to get to the valley of the Hork-Bajir. But every time I'm almost there, I get lost. East is suddenly west and north is south until, all at once, the valley appears right in front of me. And I'm never quite sure how I found it.

It was the same story this morning. I was flying in circles until, suddenly . . .

I soared over a ridge and into the first rays of the rising sun. There, before me, breathtaking as always, stretched the valley. And the stream, slowly winding its way down from the ridge. I followed the stream to the camp and alighted on a branch before dropping to the ground to demorph.

The others were already waiting.

<Hello, Prince Jake.> Ax kept his main eyes

down. His stalk eyes kept constant watch all around us. <The situation is very bad. The colony is in serious danger.>

Ever since Ax acted alone in kidnapping Visser Two from the aircraft carrier — a desperate act he hoped would make the visser call off a captured American sub scheduled to release nuclear weapons against China — he hadn't looked me straight in the eyes. And to be honest, I was almost glad.

Yeah, Ax's gamble had worked. And in a strange way I was glad he'd relieved me of having to make the decision. Of having to choose death for thousands in order to save millions.

I was proud of Ax. Mad at him, too. I missed the times when our friendship was easier. Hoped it would get better. But for now, we both kind of pretended nothing major had gone down between us.

It's what we have to do.

"Why?" I asked. "What's going on?"

Marco nodded toward Toby, the young Hork-Bajir with special powers. The "seer." She's pushing seven feet, nearly as tall as the largest male Hork-Bajir.

Most Hork-Bajir aren't terribly bright. Toby is the exception. Some Hork-Bajir say she's clairvoyant, that she sees the future before it happens. All of the free Hork-Bajir look to her for guidance and advice.

Toby stood in a circle with Ax, Marco, Cassie, and Rachel. Tobias was perched on Rachel's shoulder. The other free Hork-Bajir stood with Marco's parents, listening from a distance.

"What is it, Toby? What happened?"

"We raided a Yeerk facility yesterday, Jake," she said. "A day's journey from here. We rescued four of our people." She paused and looked down at the stream. "But one of our warriors was captured."

CHAPTER 6

An awful silence followed Toby's words.

This was bad.

Capture is the stuff of nightmares, something we all fear. Unless you immediately escape or die, it means the betrayal of everyone you love and everything you value.

Because a prisoner is infested by a Yeerk. His brain is probed. Every useful memory, all relevant knowledge, is extracted and stolen for the Yeerks to use.

The Yeerk with access to the once-free Hork-Bajir's mind would have the knowledge to lead an army to the valley. Yeah, the Ellimist made it strangely difficult to locate the valley. But with a guide, the Yeerks would absolutely find their way.

"It's a no-brainer." Marco. "Haul butt before the Yeerks attack."

"There's no other way," Cassie agreed. "Even with our help, Toby, you can't fight an army of Yeerks. They have sophisticated weapons. Lots of reinforcements. There are fewer than a hundred of you." Cassie gestured to the crowd of Hork-Bajir. "Not more than sixty of you who are fit enough and old enough to fight."

"It's not fair," Rachel said angrily.

<No,> Tobias agreed. <But what choice is there?>

Toby was silent. Her expression showed nothing. She turned to Ax.

"The forest is too thick for the effective use of Bug fighters, isn't it?" she asked. "And the valley's too narrow."

Ax's stalk eyes scanned the closely spaced trees. <That is true. But that fact only improves the odds by a very small percentage.>

Toby turned to me now. "Will you help us defend our valley, Jake? Our home?"

I was getting a little annoyed. Toby didn't seem to get it. If we tried to fight the Yeerks, we'd be slaughtered.

"We want to help," I said. "But not if it means setting you up to lose."

Toby looked up into the trees, then turned to survey the camp. She planted the stick she was holding into the yielding ground.

31

"This valley is our home," she said loudly. "We will not give it up. We'll stay and fight."

Marco threw up his hands in exasperation. "Let me understand what I'm hearing, here. You all want to die, is that it?" He looked around at the other Hork-Bajir who remained politely withdrawn from our discussion. "Don't be insane! Mom, Dad? You're with them?"

Marco's parents were as diffident as the Hork-Bajir. They stood impassive and expressionless, feet firmly planted on the hard-packed dirt.

I rubbed my forehead and tried to think. Time was running out. The Yeerks were probably already on the way. Preparations had to be made.

I climbed into the V of a nearby tree, up about ten feet so everybody in the camp could see and hear me.

"Listen!" I shouted. "The Yeerks will probably be here by tomorrow morning, the latest. They will kill or infest all of you if you don't leave right now. Everyone must prepare to move out. We'll help you find a new camp."

No one moved.

"Jake," Toby said. "No Yeerk will drive us from this home. I am willing to stay and fight and so are my people."

Grunts of accord rose from the free Hork-Bajir spectators.

I couldn't believe what I was hearing.

"Wait!" I yelled. "You know the Yeerks have advanced weapons. You've seen the Dracon beams. Save yourselves!" I looked at Toby. "Escape now. Live to fight another day!"

No one answered.

Marco strode angrily toward his parents, like he was about to give them a piece of his mind. Rachel glanced up at me with her trademark fearless look. She wanted me to reconsider.

Fine, we were taking sides. The decision would come down to a vote. I jumped from the tree.

"Come on!" I shouted, desperation pounding in my brain. "All those who want to live, stand over here with me. Those who want to die at the hands of the Yeerks, stand over there, with Toby."

There was no mumbling, no movement.

<This is your decision,> Tobias said to the Hork-Bajir. <But I think you should listen to Jake. He only wants what's best.>

"We all do," Cassie said.

I glanced at Ax. He stood a bit apart, aloof. He wasn't giving his opinion.

A serious question for Andalites, especially now for Ax. Meddle where you might not belong. Possibly save lives in the process. Or just walk away. Let a people decide its own fate.

A young Hork-Bajir stepped out from the

crowd and walked toward Toby. He stood straight and tall at her side. Jara Hamee and Ket Helpek joined him. Others followed.

Until every Hork-Bajir in the colony stood with their leader.

CHAPTER 7
Isaiah
Fitzhenry

I threw back the flap of the hospital tent and entered. Light became darkness. Cool, fresh air became a stifling, acrid stench.

The smell of sickness and death.

I moved forward, eyes straining to see.

"Ah!"

I bumped something warm and soft and drew back instantly as the object voiced a high-pitched objection.

"I beg your pardon!" I groped to find a tent pole. "Sally, is that you?"

As my eyes adjusted, I saw a woman standing over a table, wringing out a bloodstained cloth into a bowl of water.

"'Tis I, Lieutenant," Sally answered with more cheerfulness than I expected. "You'd be looking for the prisoner?"

"That I would, Sally." Sally Miller is a woman from town. If Sinkler's Ridge is worth its place on the map, it is thanks to her. We'd have lost more men by now were it not for the morale boost the men found in Sally's excellent care.

"This way," she said. "We sectioned him off so he wouldn't upset the others. He's restrained, of course, but I saw to his wound."

"You're a wonder, Sally."

"So my husband tells me on occasion. But these men need me, Lieutenant, and I believe in their cause." She pulled back a pitifully soiled sheet strung up between the tent wall and a post. "The Union cause," she emphasized, turning to leave me with the Confederate soldier who lay on the floor.

His wrists and ankles were bound. The fresh white bandage wound around the left biceps had just begun to soak through with blood.

He stared at me with defiant eyes.

"So the Union has a kid in charge," he said softly. "Yankees got a boy commander."

The derisive remark cut through my pride and struck anger. I was fully aware that I didn't look the part. I didn't need reminding.

"And yet," I answered, "my men have managed to shoot and capture you. That's not bad for child's play."

"I cut you off," he said to console himself. "With no telegraph, Yank, you're as forgotten as on a desert island. Only difference here is that you're about to take a pounding."

"Is that right?" I mocked, intentionally disbelieving.

"Darn right!" he raged. "General Forrest has five hundred troopers in Springville, plus a reserve of —"

He stopped short.

His eyes grew wide as he realized what he had done.

I now knew what the enemy's approach would likely be, their number, and their position.

"I thank you, sir," I said, bowing my head. "You have been very helpful."

He kicked the air and lunged as if to strike me, but the pain in his upper arm would not allow it. He fell back in a heap, cursing, sweating.

And I forgot my anger long enough to empathize.

This low-ranking Rebel was fighting for a cause he thought was right. For his home, his people.

He was badly mistaken.

But that didn't change his valiant spirit. Were our roles reversed, I hope I would rally in kind.

I returned the soiled sheet to its position.

"You'll be wanting to visit your own men now?" Sally asked, pointing at a canvas flap beyond which lay my men.

No, I didn't want to see them. I didn't want to see suffering I could do nothing about.

I hesitated.

"It would be good for morale," Sally urged. "And your friend, Corporal Carson, has been inquiring after you."

"Yes, of course," I said. I ducked through the canvas before I thought better of it.

The bodies of my detachment lay motionless, packed tight in the tent like sleeping sardines.

I walked down the narrow aisle, looking in vain for signs of recovery.

"Isaiah," a slender voice called from knee-level.

Mac Carson's half-open eyes looked up into mine. Corporal Carson. We'd grown up together, been schooled together, and now fought side by side. Despite the new scar on his left cheek, he looked like the boy I'd always known. Big bones, white teeth, black hair, green eyes.

I knelt and placed my hand against his forehead. It was on fire.

"What news?" he whispered.

"Twenty-five men," I said flatly. "That's all we have. Forrest's force may be over five hundred."

Mac wheezed.

"Thirty men came down from the hills this morning," I continued. "They want to fight."

"Thank God," Mac said firmly. His family was progressive on all counts, abolitionism among them. "You need the men and they've a right to fight. It's their war, too, now."

"Be rational, Mac! You sound like the little man who leads them."

"Jacob?"

"How did you know of him?" I asked, astonished.

"I met him when we came into town. He came down alone, looking for work. We shared some soft bread."

"You spoke to him?"

"I should say! He's quite educated," Mac said. "Taught himself to read and write, but hid it from his former master who would have sold him South to be sure. He never knew his mother or father. They were sold or traded or some such abominable thing."

"Has he been whipped?"

"I imagine so, though probably not often. I've sometimes thought that living life under the threat of whipping and punishment would be just as bad as the thing itself. Perhaps worse."

"I suppose," I said absently, glancing around at my lifeless men. I was almost certain that the body next to Mac had ceased to breathe.

"Can you cover my feet?" Mac asked.

I moved to the end of his cot and nearly gasped. The first two toes on either foot were bloody and brown.

"Frostbite," he said with a weak smile.

I wrapped the wool blanket around them.

"Raines doesn't think we'll be able to hold off the enemy," I said.

Mac coughed and nodded.

"Let the Negroes fight," he said.

I rose to my feet in frustration.

"Isaiah," Mac said, catching my arm. "They're our only hope."

CHAPTER 8

Jake

"They're going to fight with or without us," Cassie said, awed. As if maybe she'd suddenly changed her mind about what our role should be. "They're risking everything for their freedom."

"We have to respect that," Rachel said. "And we owe it to the Hork-Bajir to help."

I still couldn't believe what had just happened.

<This is just plain amazing,> Tobias said to us privately. <These Hork-Bajir know who they are and what they want.>

"Okay." I sighed. "We'll help you."

Marco glanced at me with a mix of exasperation and resignation. He knew this was an argument we couldn't win.

41

Cassie flashed me a look that said I'd done the right thing.

Toby smiled the strangely frightening Hork-Bajir smile.

"Tobias, as always, you're our eye in the sky. Check out the area and see if you can spot an escape route. I have a feeling we're gonna need one. Marco, get in touch with Erek. See if a few Chee can cover back home for those of us who need it."

Toby stared at me.

"If we need to escape." I corrected myself and smiled.

I began to draw a rough map of the area in the dirt with a stick. Toby walked over to where I was crouched down.

"Thank you," she said.

"Yeah, well . . . I just hope your people understand what they're getting into. It ain't gonna be pretty."

"They understand much more than you give them credit for, Jake. They've been called upon to defend themselves before. They've been through a lot."

I nodded sheepishly and looked back at the dirt map.

After a while, I ventured further into the camp to check on the battle preparations. With advice from Rachel and Ax, the Hork-Bajir were positioning platforms in the trees.

A Hork-Bajir with a bundle of small tree limbs on his back and a coil of rope in his hand would scramble up a trunk, using heel and wrist blades to climb. Like a telephone repairman in fast forward. When he'd get about thirty feet up, he'd dig his ankle blades in firmly, lock in with both knee blades, and lean back. With both hands free, he'd lash the branches together. In about ten minutes, there was an elaborate but perfectly camouflaged platform.

When the builder finished, he'd climb onto the platform to test its strength. Then he'd descend quickly, move to another tree, and begin again.

Younger Hork-Bajir then climbed to the completed platforms and stocked them with spears and arrows. Weapons the female Hork-Bajir were turning out with speed, efficiency, and skill. It was unbelievable to watch.

Hork-Bajir elders, the few who weren't quite as quick at climbing as they used to be, dug pits and trenches all over the camp. After one was dug, the very smallest Hork-Bajir children were lowered into it to place pointed wooden spikes into the dirt. Whoever fell into these holes would come out looking like Swiss cheese. If they came out at all. With the spikes in place, the kids were hauled up to help cover the pits. First with twigs that spanned the opening. Then with leaves that formed a bed to conceal it completely.

43

Satisfied as I could be under the circumstances, I called the others and Toby to the map to discuss strategy.

"We're here." I pointed to two long, parallel lines marking the narrow passage. "On either side of us are steep banks and cliffs. Impossible to climb without serious time and effort. So I think the Yeerks will come up the valley this way," I said, pointing. "From the south, uphill."

"That's good for us," Marco said.

<It will slow their approach,> Ax agreed, <but it will also interfere with our retreat. Tobias said our only escape route will be up the valley to the north.> Ax pointed to a place where the valley widened, about a mile north of the camp. <The valley walls become easier to climb at this point, but will still be slow and difficult.>

I looked at Toby.

"You'd be much better off to climb the valley walls now and fight from up there."

"We will defend our home."

<We've got another problem,> Tobias said. <I spotted a group of campers. And they're going to be in the Yeerks' way.>

"I guess we'll have to try to convince them to get out of there," I said.

Cassie put her hand on Toby's arm. "Even if you survive, you'll have to go into hiding. Where will you go?"

"If we're forced to withdraw temporarily," Toby said calmly, "we'll go to the hills."

"But the trees in the hills aren't the same kind as the ones in the valley. And they won't provide great shelter. You'll have to adapt all over again."

<And those hills are getting pretty close to the suburbs,> Tobias added. <It wouldn't be safe to hang there very long. Eventually, you'd run into some humans.>

"Maybe it's time the Hork-Bajir did run into some humans," Rachel said. "We can't count on the Ellimist to appear and help out just because we want him to. If the right people knew what was going on, all sort of things could happen — good and bad.

Marco smirked. "News flash: Your average suburbanite ain't gonna tolerate a seven-foot-tall bladed alien for a neighbor. I mean, carpooling? Toby as a soccer mom? Think about it."

Toby's eyes dropped.

"I'm sorry. We don't think of you as freaks, but the average guy on the street? Toby, humans can't even deal with other humans who root for a rival football team."

"Yes," Toby said slowly. "I've learned that humans don't care for groups unlike their own."

"That's not always true," I said.

<My study of human history suggests that

45

Marco and Toby are both correct,> Ax said carefully. <Historically, humans are among the least tolerant species in the galaxy, set apart by the prevalence of violence and oppression."

"So, what would you suggest, Ax?" Cassie asked. "Send the Hork-Bajir to some distant planet? All because humans are tolerance-challenged? That can't be the only answer."

"It stinks," Marco said. "But take a look at what humans have done to animals. If there's a chance to dominate, we grab it. I'd rather be a tiger or elephant on Neptune than a striped rug or an ivory box on Earth. The farther away you can get, Toby, the better off you'll be."

For a moment, Toby said nothing.

"But are we really that different from you?" she said finally.

She turned toward camp. Toward a Hork-Bajir who bent low to the ground and scooped her crying child into her arms.

The child had fallen. The mother carefully raised the child to her shoulder and gently patted its back.

No, the Hork-Bajir weren't really that different at all.

CHAPTER 9
Isaiah
Fitzhenry

At sundown, Sergeant Raines and two other soldiers walked with me down the main street of Sinkler's Ridge.

Sally Miller and her husband, Joe, were hosting a Christmas party. They'd been kind enough to invite us and we were happy to oblige.

I detailed a number of men for picket duty and left Sergeant Spears in command until our return. Our pickets were spread out through the woods and hills skirting the town. Before the enemy attacked, we would be alerted.

Several townsmen, Joe Miller among them, brought their own shovels and picks and joined us in the digging this afternoon. They wouldn't work near the black men, nor even within sight of

47

them. They said Jacob's men were a disgrace to the Union.

Perhaps. But no one can deny the progress they made. Trees covering the entire south face of Topper Hill were felled and left lying, a formidable defense when time is short.

And the Negroes shaped the earthworks like seasoned engineers. Most of the men dug all afternoon, and would dig all day tomorrow.

We stopped before a white clapboard house with candles flickering warmly in the windows. Fiddle music filtered through the walls and under the door. I climbed the stairs and let the knocker fall.

Scents of cinnamon and vanilla rushed out as the door opened. Sally greeted us warmly. "Lieutenant. Hello, Raines. Welcome."

Sally was resplendent with golden hair bouncing in ringlets and a red-trimmed dress to match her lips. She stepped back to let us enter and nodded as we passed.

We were drawn in by the sound of music and voices. Raines hastened to the banjo case that stood in the corner, threw it open, and pulled out the instrument like a child opening a gift on Christmas morning.

Private Tweed raised a tambourine. Corporal Fox unsheathed a pair of bones from his jacket pocket. No words were exchanged. They simply joined the town fiddler, then started in on a new song, the words of which I'd heard before.

"I hear the bugle sound the calls
for reveille and drill,
for water, stable, and tattoo,
for taps — and all was still.
I hear it sound the Sick-Call grim,
and see the men in line,
with faces wry as they drink down
their whiskey and quinine."

The stress of the impending attack seemed to melt away. The townspeople present clapped and tapped their feet in time. The young tin whistler and drummer boy, the two I'd seen out my drafty window, watched from beside the roaring fire.

"Good evening, Lieutenant," Joe Miller said. "Merry Christmas." He was a broad man, built for agricultural life. His beard and mustache were even redder than his hair. His wide smile matched his frame.

"And to you, Miller," I answered. "As you see, my men are glad to put aside their duties."

"Come." Miller took me by the arm and led me to a long table by the window. "Sample the foods my Sally has prepared."

My mouth dropped open at the sight.

Spread across the table were the foods I dreamed of at night. Milk, cheese, cake, preserves, boiled ham, turkey, pudding, pickles, and loaves of fresh-baked soft bread.

"Eat up," Miller said. "Maintain the strength you need to save this town."

I reached for a buttery cinnamon roll.

"I wish that I alone could save it," I said solemnly. "As you know, our ranks are thin. We may need to arm the men that came into camp today. They're willing to fight, and they —"

"Are you mad?!" The joviality drained from Miller's face. He bellowed as though addressing a plow horse.

"I assure you I am not," I said quietly.

Raines appeared beside me at the buffet table. The song had finished. The guests were clapping loudly.

Miller appealed to Raines.

"Your lieutenant says he would arm a band of runaway Negroes and let them fight the Rebels," Miller said, forcing unwilling laughter from his throat and patting Raines on the back. "Is he a jokester, Raines? Or does he take to the bottle in the evening?"

"I assure you, sir," I said, loudly enough to silence some of the guests. "There is no joke intended, nor any drunkenness among the detachment."

Miller's face grew still, like a bull before the charge.

"Once you arm those Negroes, what stops them from running wild?"

"Have you met the men, sir?" I said.

"I wouldn't go within fifty feet of those people. I don't need to meet a wolf to know he'll cause all kinds of mischief. They'll take our chickens, our pigs, the house!"

"The Rebels will do far worse if they take the town. The Negroes have offered to help. They've offered their lives."

"If you treat them as equals, Lieutenant, they'll begin to believe it." The color in Miller's face was rising. "For God's sake! If you let them fight, they'll begin to believe they deserve other liberties. Where would it go from there? Would you have them living here in Sinkler's Ridge? In a house on Main Street?"

Chuckles rippled through the group of townspeople, most of whom had stopped their chatter now to listen in.

Mac once told me integration was the course of the future, the only way.

"You believe peaceful coexistence to be impossible?" I asked, knowing Miller's answer.

"Darn right I do!"

"Joe, calm yourself!" Sally cautioned.

Raines spoke. "Lieutenant, these men, they've

never been trained. They'll only get in the way." The objection was a practical one. Raines can always be relied upon for pragmatism. "Besides, at the first shot, they'll run."

"I think you're wrong, Raines," I said plainly.

"*You* are wrong, Lieutenant," Miller argued. "The people of Sinkler's Ridge are of one mind on this issue." He waved a hand to include the observing group of guests.

Heads nodded.

"If you persist in this absurd support of slaves, you'll find that our support will disappear," Miller said stiffly.

Sally turned abruptly and walked from the room. She understood her husband's meaning but obviously did not approve.

"Come, men," I said. Fox and Tweed rose from their chairs. "It seems we've outstayed our welcome."

We left the warm, white house for the cold, black night and walked in silence to the camp.

Spears reported that the pickets had seen nothing but trees in the woods and hills.

I climbed into my narrow makeshift bed and closed my eyes.

All I saw were the colorful foods on the buffet table, the orange fire roaring in the hearth, and Sally's smiling eyes.

And all I heard was music.

CHAPTER 10
Jake

The more I looked at the makeshift map, the more I realized there weren't going to be any Hork-Bajir left to relocate after the Yeerks came through.

I saw the battle in my mind. I saw the scouts storm the encampment and fire their Dracon beams on everything that moved. I saw the swarm of Taxxons. Hundreds of unstoppable mouths devouring anything with a pulse.

We could slow the Yeerks, inflict sufficient casualties to make the visser in charge look bad. But in the end, defeat was inevitable.

The thought of a total slaughter made me sick.

I had to get away, get another look. Maybe there was something I'd missed.

I morphed peregrine falcon and flew down the valley to the south. The valley was like a wind tunnel. A steady stream of rushing air that kept me aloft almost as well as a thermal.

My raptor eyes caught a flash of movement, something bright and oddly colored in the forest. I banked and dove, soaring close over the treetops. Through the canopy of leaves and branches, a cluster of tents. Three blue, one green, one yellow, one purple. I banked again and made another pass.

A group of sixteen people. Four adults and a bunch of mostly high school kids. The campers Tobias had told us about.

I dropped through the trees. I could smell meat cooking, hot dogs I think, and singed marshmallows. I landed and my talons bit firmly into the branch of a fallen tree.

I was less than fifty feet from the group. I could see everything. Camping equipment scattered everywhere. Metal plates and pans. Boots and wool socks drying on tree branches. Open backpacks, spilling their contents of brightly colored camping gear onto the dirt.

Given the amounts of garbage the campers had strung up in the tree branches, beyond the reach of bears, they'd been camped for more than three days. Unless these people had portable Kandrona pools in their tiny tents, they weren't Controllers.

I gave in to an irresistible urge to preen and caught the eye of a man in a puffy yellow vest. Watched him magnify and focus a pair of field glasses, then show the kid standing next to him.

I looked directly at them.

We had to get the campers out of there.

I flew up along the edge of the valley and along the crest of the hill north of the colony. Followed the stream that flowed down the valley, through the colony and beyond.

WWHUUMPH!

A small tree toppled. Rustled the brush along the stream.

Who would be chopping down trees out here?

I doubled back and landed on the top of a high pine. The small tree had fallen into the water. Not into the rushing stream itself, but into an adjoining pond.

I watched as two small brown heads pushed and tugged on the tree until it moved swiftly through the water toward the edge of the pond. Until it became entangled in a pile of other wood and debris.

One of the animals lumbered up onto the bank. It was three feet long, covered in slick brown fur. A long, flat, paddle-shaped tail dragged along behind it.

Beavers damming the stream.

The wall of wood and brush that held back

the pond was leaking. The beavers were working hard to fix it. If the wall broke, all that dammed-up water would rush down the hillside, into the Hork-Bajir colony, and on through the valley floor.

It was too good to be true.

A wall of water rushing toward the colony, funneling toward the attacking Yeerks?

I checked the size of the pond, and the distance the water had to travel to reach the colony and valley floor beyond . . .

No good.

The water in the pond would spread out and diminish by the time it reached the Yeerks. It would spill over the banks of the stream and rage for a while. But where it mattered, it would end up as little more than a puddle.

My brilliant idea began to die. I was about to fly away when the beavers pushed another cluster of tangled branches into position. The wall rose higher. The water level raised ever so slightly.

That's when it hit me.

If two beavers could dam a pond, five beavers could dam a whole lot more.

CHAPTER 11

"We're going to flood them out," I announced. "We're going to wash the Yeerks back down the valley.

The beavers have already started things for us. We just have to expand their dam to hold back enough water to make a mini tidal wave."

"Nap time!" Marco sang. "I think someone's a *little* overtired."

"I'm fine."

Tobias laughed. <You know, this mission is seriously important. I'm thinking the morph should be a little more, I don't know, glamorous. I mean, going beaver to save an entire colony of aliens is like putting James Bond behind the

57

wheel of a minivan. With a bumper sticker that says, "World's Greatest Mom." No offense.>

"Very funny. Listen, we've gone mole. We've gone ant. You use what works."

"But will this work?" Rachel asked.

"Got any other ideas?" I answered.

We didn't have to morph to travel to the beaver dam. It was only about an eight-minute jog up the valley. As we approached the pond . . .

Whack! Whack! Sploosh! Sploosh!

Thundering slaps loud as firecrackers, and no beavers to be seen. New ripples crossed the pond.

"They must have heard us coming," Cassie said. "Beavers slap their tails on the water if they think they're in danger."

The pond looked promising. It was bigger than it had seemed from the air.

Attached to a lake, it would have made a respectable fishing cove.

In my backyard, it would have made a fantastic swimming pool.

But I knew we needed more. I just didn't know how much.

<Three to four thousand cubic meters,> Ax said. <I believe that is what it will take to inundate the valley.>

Marco batted his eyelashes. "Ax, you just make me all tingly when you talk all smart-like."

"How much water is that?" I asked.

"We have to make this pool Olympic-sized," Marco answered.

A beaver popped up in the middle of the pond, pushing a branch with his nose. He placed the branch in the dam and dove back underwater.

We waited. And waited.

<Some lungs,> Tobias observed.

"No," Cassie explained, "he's probably in the lodge. See that dome-shaped pile of branches and moss and mud sticking up above water level? There's air in there."

"The lodge?" Marco echoed excitedly. "A roaring fire. Hot chocolate. Britney Spears. Brandy, maybe. The girl, not the drink. These dudes know how to live!"

"The lodge is where they live," Cassie laughed. "Like bears have dens and birds have nests?"

"How do we acquire a beaver while he's inside the lodge?" Rachel said.

Cassie waded into the water. "Well, the entrances are underwater," she said. "Maybe we can catch a beaver on his way out."

She reached the lodge and bent down toward its base. Murky water slapped her chin.

"Found it," she said. "I think. Someone knock lightly on the side of the lodge to scare a beaver out."

"Are you kidding?" Marco said, wading after her into the water. Rachel, Ax, and I followed. "Gentle, thoughtful Cassie wants to scare a beaver out of its mind?"

"Shut up and help. I'm not going to hurt him."

Marco tapped the lodge with a fallen branch.

"Got him!" Cassie cried. "Oowwwww! He bit me!"

"Cassie, let go!"

"I'm okay," she said quickly. Then she lifted the beaver to the surface. His body was still from the acquiring trance, buoyed weight.

Good thing, because this guy had to weigh at least forty pounds, big and sturdy. The body of an industrious worker. One by one, including Tobias, we reached out to touch the slick, bristly coat.

The beaver splashed away as soon as we were done.

"You know," Cassie said, forcing a smile, blood dripping from the cut on her hand, "when your mother tells you not to stick your hand in a beaver lodge, you really should listen."

CHAPTER 12

Isaiah Fitzhenry

December 24, 1864.

Joe Miller's rooster crowed at half past five, leaving no question that it had survived the night despite his predictions of raid and plunder by the Negros.

While the coffee boiled, I rummaged in my haversack for sugar. I found none, I had to drink my coffee black.

It felt like an ominous omen.

"Don't lag, men. Don't lag!"

Sergeant Spears's husky voice roared through the frigid air. As I made my way across the stream and down the hill, I saw him standing statuesque in the morning fog, having staked out the highest point of the earthworks to supervise

Jacob and the other men, who labored dutifully below.

Spears's rifle was propped against his shoulder. That was as it should have been, for I'd ordered all men to carry arms on every detail.

But from my vantage point, Spears seemed to have his hand rather too close to the trigger.

"They're lazy men, Lieutenant," Spears said, far too loudly, as he saw me approaching. "If our men was out working, we'd have finished by now."

"The problem as I see it, Spears, is that the earth is frozen hard as granite."

"No, sir," Spears said, chuckling, his Scottish accent lengthening his vowels in a most defiant way. "The earth is soft as butter, ain't it, boys? Soft as creamy butter."

Jacob looked up, saw me, and dropped his shovel on the dirt.

"Lieutenant!" he called, waving an arm and pushing toward me over piles of upturned soil. "I want to speak to you about —"

"You!" Spears bellowed.

Jacob froze.

"Resume your position and your duty!"

Jacob hesitated.

"Lieutenant," he called to me. "It's about the placement of the —"

BAM!

A rifle shot cracked the air.

Jacob hit the ground.

Spears began to chuckle again. He had fired into the sky.

"Spears!" I yelled.

He returned the gun to his shoulder. Jacob staggered to his feet. The eyes of all the black men turned to me.

"Yes, sir?" Spears answered.

"Ride out to scout for the enemy. Take a few men with you."

"Are you relieving me of this detail?"

"I will stand in until your return."

"Very well, sir."

Spears scampered down the earthworks and strode past me in silence. Though he was my subordinate, I couldn't very well question his behavior in front of the men. I had to back him.

"Back to work, men!" I yelled. "Jacob, approach!" I said sternly, and retained a posture of severity until Spears was safely out of earshot.

I sensed the reason Jacob wanted to speak to me. The placement of the entrenchments was all wrong. I'd realized it, too. If we moved them back a hundred yards toward town, we could place them behind the stream, a natural barrier to the Rebs. A God-made moat.

"Jacob," I said gently. "You have an opinion to share?"

He nodded.

"Yes . . . Lieutenant. This ain't the best position. Rebs coming up from down there. Make 'em come all the way up, close to town. That way, you have more chance to shoot 'em down. Then, when they get to the stream, that slows them down some more."

"I think you're right," I said.

Spears and three privates trampled down the hill on horseback. When they reached the stream, Spears's horse reared up and whinnied loudly.

"Bronco!" Spears cried.

The horse finally plunged into the water, stepping awkwardly over rocks and mud.

Jacob and I exchanged a glance of understanding. The stream was the barrier we needed.

"Start your men digging again," I said. "But this time, according to your plan."

I waited for Jacob to accept the new orders.

"How about rifles?" he said instead, hope flickering in his eyes.

"Why are you so set on fighting? Once you prepare these entrenchments, you can melt back into the hills and be safe. Haven't you heard what these same troopers did at Fort Pillow? Don't you know the name of Nathan Bedford Forrest?"

Jacob's face grew hard and still. He did know the name. But I would drive home the reality.

"Right here in Tennessee, just over those hills a few days, General Forrest's Confederate cavalry captured a Union-held fort on the Mississippi. The Negro soldiers inside surrendered. But Forrest didn't take them prisoner. He murdered them in cold blood. Jacob, it was a massacre."

"I know, Lieutenant. If they take us, they'll most likely kill us, too."

His calm sent chills down my spine. He knew the truth, yet wanted to fight in spite of it.

"The townspeople won't allow it," I said, changing tacks. "Neither will many of my own men. You know Spears. He won't fight beside you."

Jacob looked at me stubbornly.

"You need men," he said, echoing his words from the day before. "Here we are."

I looked angrily at the camp and the town. Didn't Jacob see it was an impossibility? Yes, we were outnumbered. Yes, we needed his men. Yes, it was suicide to turn him down.

"Give us a chance, Lieutenant."

Wagons loaded with household treasures stood outside several houses in town. The white townspeople were loading their possessions and preparing to flee.

I looked at Joe and Sally Miller's house. There was no wagon there.

Clop-clop. Clop-clop. Clop-clop.

The pounding of hooves!

Spears's red and sweating face, flailing coat, and screaming horse reared up before me.

"Lieutenant!" he cried. "They're not a mile from here!"

CHAPTER 13

Jake

I put Ax in charge of the "dam expansion." He had a clear sense of the mechanics of the whole thing. Said something about how the natural curve of the beaver's dam was actually the most efficient shape to hold back the water.

"Fluid mechanics was one of my specialties as an *aristh*," Ax said.

Marco sighed. "What haven't you done?"

"I have never constructed an organic cellulose hydrological attack assemblage."

"We speak English, dude."

"No, I get it," Rachel said excitedly. "He's never made a dam out of wood, mud, and moss."

Cassie was concerned about the beaver family whose compound we were about to take over.

"They're scared. They think we're predators. We need to convince them we're friends."

"What we need to do," Marco said, "is expand this dam and store up a whole lot of water. Fast."

Marco morphed. There was a big splash as he dropped into the water. A resounding crack as he slapped his tail.

<Awesome!> he shouted. <These front teeth are great. Let me at some trees, baby! I'm gonna build me a dam.>

Cassie morphed next. Then Rachel. The beaver was kind of cute, except for the small beady eyes. And the enlarged front incisors, like curving ivory chisels.

I later learned that beaver incisors never stop growing. If the beaver doesn't wear them down with use, they grow right down to the ground.

<There is the beginning of a small canal on the far side of the pond,> Ax said. <It leads to a growth of young trees, some of which have already been cut down. We need that material for the construction. Rachel and Cassie, stay with me. Marco?>

<On my way.>

Tobias and I had other business. I morphed, and together we flew out of range of the construction below. It was a short flight to the campsite. We were careful to land far enough away so that no one would see us demorph and morph in Tobias's case.

Then we walked toward the brightly colored tents. Thank God we could finally morph some halfway decent clothes, the result of a whole lot of experience. Boys in T-shirts and jeans generally look a lot saner than boys in spandex.

We approached the campsite. A tall kid with glasses spotted us first.

"Hi," he said.

"Hey," I answered.

Then we just stood there.

<Jake? Fearless leader? Do you have a plan, or are you just going to smile and look stupid in our morphing outfits?> Tobias said privately.

"Just be cool. I'll handle it," I whispered. "I'm Jake," I said to the tall kid.

"Lewis Carpenter. I've had blisters for five days."

"Huh. Bummer."

An adult stuck his head out of a tent. The guy who had sighted me in his binoculars. "What are you two boys doing so far out in the woods?" he asked, stepping outside. "Where's your equipment?"

<Good question, Jake.>

"We're camped on the ridge," I said easily, pointing up the valley wall.

"Right," Tobias added.

More silence and staring. This was getting ridiculous.

"Look," I said. "We came to tell you we all have to get out of here. We just met a ranger and he told us the park is closed. There's a huge storm coming this way. Guy said they're predicting straight-line winds and tons of snow, enough to strand us all. Everyone's got to pack up and get out of the area before sundown."

A girl stood up from the group of kids sitting around the campfire and came closer to us. She was maybe Tom's age.

"It never snows this early in the year."

"Yeah, I know," I said quickly. "That's what's so dangerous about this storm. No one's prepared. I mean, who's gonna have cold-weather gear? Right?"

The girl grinned.

"I'll be fine. I hiked Mount McKinley."

"Emily, Lewis?" The adult binocular guy. "Let me handle this."

<They're not buying it,> Tobias said privately.

"Frostbite is bad news," I said, trying to sound all serious and worried.

"Look," said binocular guy, "you boys need to learn a thing or two about hikers' etiquette. People need to trust one another in the wilderness. You don't make up stories just to get someone else's campsite."

70

The guy held out a tiny portable television flickering a commercial for an SUV.

"The local news meteorologist predicts sunny skies and no wind for the next three days." His voice bristled with adult annoyance. And with confidence. "We're staying right where we are."

I could feel my ears getting hot. They turn red sometimes when I'm embarrassed.

Three more adults, two women and a man, came from their tents. Asked the kids what was going on. I started to feel a little sick. Like I was going to get sent to my room or earn a week's worth of detention.

"Listen," Tobias said loudly, "you have to believe us. If you don't get out of this valley now, something really bad is going to happen. Your lives are in danger."

The campers didn't respond. Emily looked at Lewis, then at the man. A kid near the campfire started to laugh. Pretty soon, all sixteen people in camp were snickering. Four adults and twelve kids, laughing at the two pathetic losers.

"Get a life," Emily said.

I turned to Tobias. "Okay. We're desparate. I don't want to do this, but I don't think we have a choice."

"Are you sure?" Tobias whispered. "What if one of them bolts? Or attacks us? Or runs straight to the local media? If the Yeerks hear that two human boys were morphing . . ."

"I know, Tobias," I snapped. "I know there are consequences."

That was my job. To know the consequences. It was also my job to make the tough decisions. To lead.

I started to morph.

"It's okay," Tobias called. "What you're going to see will shock you, but don't panic. We're only trying to help."

Lewis was the first to react. He clutched at his glasses and stepped back. Groped behind him with his free hand until he bumped into a tree. His mouth hung wide open.

The man dropped his television in the leaves. His face went white.

One boy by the campfire stumbled to his feet, then took off into the woods.

"Don't be frightened," Tobias repeated.

Morphing is not pretty. It's disturbing and grotesque. Of course the campers were frightened. Anybody would be.

My human body began to twist violently. Big, flesh-tearing teeth sprouted from my gums. Ears migrated to the top of my head. Shoulders hunched, spine expanded, skin toughened. Fur, orange with black stripes, spread across my flesh like liquid spilled out of a jar. Until finally, I fell forward onto the dirt. All five hundred pounds of me.

I was a male Siberian tiger standing before a group of whining, whimpering campers, in a place no Siberian tiger should be.

I growled gently. Just enough to let them know the tiger was real.

When Tobias started to demorph, I began to demorph to human.

Emily backed up, tripped, fell to the forest floor. Tears streaked her face.

The red-tailed hawk shrieked once, then morphed to human.

"Who . . . what are you?" the man cried.

"Its a long story," I said, fully human again. "I can't explain it all now, but you've got to believe we're not here to hurt you."

The campers were silent. At least no one else ran.

"Sometime before tomorrow noon," I said solemnly, "an army of aliens is going to march up this valley. If you're still here, they'll kill every single one of you."

CHAPTER 14

Isaiah Fitzhenry

My heart stopped.

Spears gasped for breath.

"Not a mile from here! A good-sized detachment of Forrest's cavalry. A hundred or more."

"Sound the alarm!" I ordered. "Get the men down here with everything we've got! Bayonets, muskets, revolvers . . . Spears, we're not ready for them."

Spears raced toward camp with a desperate look in his eye.

Jacob was running down the hill to rejoin the digging men. They were still building up the defensive position.

"Jacob!" I shouted above the bugle cry. "You've done your part. Get your fellows out of here!"

My men on picket duty were streaming from the woods now, hollering and whooping, running toward the earthworks like the devil was at their heels.

Jacob picked up his shovel.

"I'll be staying, Lieutenant."

He was a fool!

The men from camp raced from their tents and rushed down the hill. They pulled on coats and parkas as they came, and fastened bayonets to muskets.

"Take up your posts!" Raines cried, pulling a pistol from his belt. "Take aim, but do not fire!"

One by one, the men in blue fell into line behind the earthworks. Raines, Spears, Roth, O'Connell, McDonnell, Price . . .

We were pitifully few.

"Dear God," I breathed, drawing my own revolver.

A Rebel drum beat in the woods. General Forrest was upon us.

I watched the trees.

The tree trunks suddenly multiplied, doubling . . . tripling in number!

"Hold!" I cried, uncertain of the visual effect.

All at once, the illusion vanished and I knew what it was that I saw.

The forest was dense with brown horses, gray-coated cavalrymen, and dully reflective carbines.

"Lieutenant." Raines turned to me. "They're forming up for a charge!"

Jacob and his men were still piling up dirt. Still digging.

"Get down, you fools!" I yelled. "You'll be shot!"

A few of the men lay down against the dirt. One took off up the hill toward camp.

But Jacob and the rest ignored my warning.

"Prepare to fire. . . ."

The woods erupted with whoops and shouts. Angry cries.

"Yeeeeeee! Hah! Yooooop! Yeeeeeeeeeeeha!"

The Rebel yell.

"I'll answer you with lead!" Spears shouted down his gun barrel.

The Rebs pulled out of the woods. Numbering only fifty or so, they screamed as loud as a regiment.

The galloping hooves grew louder and louder. The whoops and hollers tortured my ears.

The Rebels jumped the trunks of the slashed trees, leaped over branches until they were so near I could almost see their faces.

I could almost see the whites of their eyes. . . .

I stepped up to the line and aimed my revolver at a snarling blond cavalryman who raised his carbine at me.

The order was rumbling inside my mind . . . waiting to explode!

"FIRE!" I raged.

"FIRE!" boomed the Rebel commander.

The Union line pulled twenty-four triggers and riddled the air with lead.

The Rebels replied in kind.

"Ahh!"

Blood spattered my face and sleeve. Private Foster clutched his neck. Blood poured through his fingers. He slumped and fell to the cold ground.

"Ahhh!"

A Negro was struck in the chest! He hit the dirt and rolled, screaming. Still, Jacob didn't take cover. He raised his shovel like a weapon.

"RELOAD!"

I hit my target in the thigh, but he kept galloping. I shot again. Missed!

Two Rebel horses down! A man falling from his mount.

"FIRE!"

My men shot again before the Rebels could reload, a difficult task while riding.

Three Rebs down on the east flank. Six or more on the west.

"BAYONETS!" I cried. No time for another shot. I picked up Foster's musket and gripped it hard. Fire coursed through my veins.

The hooves grew thunderous, racing, pounding. Roaring up to the earthworks!

"FORWARD!" I ordered.

We stabbed the air, whooping like banshees.

The Rebel horses faltered, reared up. The riders struggled to draw their sabers, but too late! We were upon them!

Union men stabbed through Rebel trousers, pulled bodies from horses. Everywhere I looked, punching, stabbing, beating.

One Rebel cleared his saber of its sheath.

And skewered O'Connell.

"STEADY, BOYS!" I ran for the man I'd struck with my revolver. I didn't realize until too late . . .

BAM!

He'd saved his carbine shot for me!

"Ahh!"

The bullet struck my stomach, threw me back!

I hit the dirt and clutched my stomach. No air!

The Rebel snarled, turned, and retreated.

No air!

My head was empty and full, calm and crazy. . . .

"Lieutenant!"

It was Jacob's voice. He told his men to drag me back behind the entrenchments.

Strong hands clasped my arms, lifted, raised me off the ground.

All around, men locked in combat with the Rebs who'd fallen from their mounts.

The Rebs on horseback were broken up, scattering to retreat.

Jacob heaved his shovel like a javelin. It struck a Rebel in the side. The man slumped and slid off the saddle.

Four of the other men swarmed another cavalryman and dragged him off his horse.

The men carrying me placed me on the ground and raced away to aid their fellows.

I ripped open my coat and groped my stomach, searching for the injury. My ribs and guts felt crushed and broken, but there was no blood, no bullet, no hole at all!

How!

My head was swimming. Footsteps stopped beside me. I looked up and saw Joe Miller's face against the sky. He had a shotgun in his hand, a revolver in his belt, a knife in his boot. He smiled and picked up the brass belt buckle I'd just thrown off.

It was utterly deformed, nearly cut in two, and folded up around a point at its center.

He handed me the buckle and I saw the flattened lead bullet embedded in the buckle.

"You're a lucky man, Lieutenant. That buckle is lead-lined."

I'd been shot in the gut and survived. No words would form.

"Those slaves," Joe Miller said. "I'll give them credit for determination." He glanced at the battlefield, at the Union men rounding up Rebel prisoners, then looked back at me.

"This was just a slight effort," I said hoarsely. "A testing of our defense. The Rebs will be back soon."

Miller nodded.

"That's why you need the help of every man you can find," he said, looking at the Negros. "Arm them, train them, and let them fight."

CHAPTER 15

Jake

The campers believed.

The initial terror on their faces softened to looks of curiosity and recognition. An adult retrieved the kid who'd run off into the woods. The rest glanced at one another, then back at us, and, suddenly, began to beam.

I didn't get it.

"We'll follow your instructions," one of the men said. About twelve of the others nodded in agreement.

<Okay. That was too easy,> Tobias said privately.

The man who'd spoken stepped delicately toward us. As if the snap of a branch would make us disappear.

"I've waited my entire life to make contact," he said suddenly. "My name is Richard Carpenter. What do you call yourselves? What system do you call home?"

"What system?"

"What solar system are you from? Are you with the Federation? Is your ship in orbit or on land?"

Unbelievable. I almost laughed.

"Uh," I said, "we're from Earth, just like you."

"Ah, yes," Richard said. "I always knew you lived among us. I have friends who've seen your ships."

"We don't have any ships," Tobias said.

Richard reached out, grasped Tobias's hand, and pumped it in a too-long handshake. Then he grabbed my hand.

"I'm honored to meet you. So very, very, very honored."

"Can you become anything you want?" Lewis said.

"No, not anything, but a lot of things. Any animal we touch," I said.

Yeah, morphing was gross and uncomfortable. But it had been a long time since I remembered it was also very, very cool.

Lewis grinned. "So, like, what's your natural form?"

"We're just normal kids with a special power," Tobias said carefully. "We're not aliens."

"If you don't want us to call you aliens, we won't call you aliens," Richard said with a wink.

<Jake? These people spend way too much time watching *Star Wars*.>

"Look," I said. "There are aliens taking over Earth, but we're just regular kids. You know, from here. Trying to stop them. The bad aliens."

Emily's forehead scrunched with skeptical wrinkles.

"It's a long story." Tobias sighed. "Just trust us. Please. You need to get out of here."

"Can't you just beam us somewhere else?" Lewis asked.

"Or you could generate a shield to surround us," said another kid with spiky blond hair and sunglasses. "You could cloak our entire campsite so we could watch all the action!"

"Yeah!" That was one of the adult women.

"Okay, look," I said, fed up. "This is real life. This is not a *Star Trek* episode. I'm not Captain Picard. I can't beam you anywhere."

"Justin," Richard said to the blond kid. "They can't put that kind of technology in our hands. It would violate the Prime Directive."

"Oh, right," Justin whispered loudly. "Of course."

Richard looked at me.

"I know that revealing yourselves to us is a major violation of the Prime Directive. But you did the right thing. We're ready for contact."

Tobias snorted.

"Are you official Trekkies or something?"

"Actually, yeah." Emily blushed. "Our parents, too, like my dad here," she said, pointing at Richard. "This is the annual camping trip. You know, a few days away from computers and videos and stuff."

"So you're not with the Federation?" Richard pressed.

Tobias and I helped break camp. In less than an hour everyone had assembled, packs on their backs.

"You need to take the quickest path out of the valley," I explained. "The Yeerks will be coming from the south, so you can't go that way."

"Who are the Yeerks?" Emily asked.

I looked at Tobias. He shrugged, then nodded.

"I'll tell you," I said, "but you have to promise not to tell anyone about anything you've seen or heard tonight. Secrecy is essential. For your safety and ours. For the, uh, Federation. Can we count on you?"

"Absolutely," said a female adult. "If there's one thing we can do, it's keep an intergalactic secret."

I ignored the knot in my stomach. I was taking a risk with these people and I knew that. Their lives were in my hands. But times were desperate. Things had changed.

"Okay. The Yeerks are parasites. In their natural form they're just slugs. Pretty much blind, deaf, and dumb. They need bodies through which they can live and be powerful. So they invade the brains of other species. Like Hork-Bajir."

"Hork-Bajir?" Lewis repeated.

"A naturally harmless group of aliens. Almost completely enslaved by the Yeerks. The Yeerks are coming to destroy the small colony of free Hork-Bajir in this valley and infest any survivors."

"'Infest'?" Justin.

"Yeah, infest," I said. "The Yeerks crawl into your head through your ear canal. Then they attach themselves to your brain. Enslave you. Take total control of your mind. You become what we call a Controller. A prisoner in your own head. Basically, you can say good-bye to free will. The Yeerk totally manipulates you to get other bodies for other Yeerks."

Justin made a face. "Why don't people just say, like, no to these Controllers?"

"It's not that easy," Tobias said. "Controllers look and act just like you and me, which makes them seriously dangerous. Look, the Yeerks are all about betrayal. No one can be trusted."

"No one," I emphasized. "Not neighbors, not relatives, not friends. That's why you need to keep your mouths shut about what you've just seen. And about anything else you might see. Because if a Controller overhears you, you're history."

<Nice try,> Tobias said dryly. <But you know someone's going to blab.>

"Well, I want to help," Emily declared. "We have to free the Hork-Bajir and crush the Yeerks!"

Tobias grinned. "Remind you of anyone, Jake?"

"Yeah," Lewis said. "Let's help the good aliens!"

"Wait," Richard cried. "Your mother would have a fit."

Lewis grabbed his dad's arm.

"Real aliens, Dad."

Richard looked down at his son's glowing face.

"You're right, kid," he declared. "It's a once-in-a-lifetime chance. We'll join your fight!"

Tobias shot me a glance. <Jake, they just don't get it yet. You need to get graphic.>

"I don't think you understand what this means," I said, looking hard at each camper.

"We're talking real battle. Real war. Pain and blood and even death," I said. "Spilled guts and severed limbs and psychological horror you won't ever get past. This isn't a trip to a theme park. It's not TV or some video game. It's an appointment with a seriously grim reality."

"I understand," Justin said. "And I'm going home. Sorry, guys, but I'm no hero." He handed Lewis a small black case. "Take some pictures, okay, Lew? This stuff sounds perfect for our Web page."

"Secrecy, remember!" I barked.

Justin looked startled. "Oh. Right."

Then two other campers walked off with him.

The remaining thirteen, it seemed, were coming with us.

<Is this smart?> Tobias said. <I mean, can we do this? Can we take these people to the free Hork-Bajir? Can we involve them this way?>

"We already have. And besides," I reasoned pathetically, "no one will believe reports of aliens from a bunch of Trekkies. I hope."

We led the thirteen campers, ten kids and three adults, the mile or so back to the Hork-Bajir settlement.

We approached the outskirts of the colony. A dozen Hork-Bajir, eerily visible in the flickering torchlight, stood in two rows on either side of the path. Toby stood in the middle.

"Welcome," she said. "We're honored by your presence. We thank you for your help."

The campers didn't speak. They just walked on through the canopy of branches and the towering, bladed extraterrestrials.

"How did you know we were coming?" I asked Toby.

"The trees whispered something about new friends who would take up our cause. Human friends who would join our fight," she said. "I see things, Jake. Many things."

CHAPTER 16

Isaiah
Fitzhenry

All told, the Union lost five men, the Rebels thirteen.

It was fine fighting by our side. Accurate shooting and brave hand-to-hand.

But we know it was a gift. A sweet, ephemeral moment of triumph.

Forrest's cavalry will return and in full force.

I do believe that anticipation of an event can be as powerful as the event itself, as Mac had said of whipping. We don't know when the attack will come and we surely can't prevent it. Yet we can live it in our minds a hundred times.

Sinkler's Ridge is doomed.

Everyone is aware of this truth, but no one will let on. Not even for a moment.

"Atten-SHUN!"

I stared into the black faces of nearly thirty men. Their bodies stiffened tall before me. The sun beat down from the zenith of its path, but its rays weren't sufficient to warm us. Misted breath billowed and steamed from the noses and mouths of men seething with excitement.

For they had just been armed.

The rifles of the sick men, the rifles of the dead — together they numbered just enough.

One of the Negros, a young man with a square jaw, couldn't contain himself.

"I wish my massa could see me now!"

He raised the rifle and made as if to shoot the older Negro next to him.

"Atten-SHUN!" I repeated, stepping closer to the line.

The young one lowered the weapon to his side and fixed an obedient stare on a distant point.

"This is not a toy!" I snapped. "What's your name?"

"Samson," he answered, avoiding my gaze.

"Do you know what you hold at your side?"

"A weapon, sir?"

"The model '61 Springfield musket with rifled bore and socket bayonet," I clarified for all to hear. I gripped my own weapon tightly. "Nine pounds and fifty-eight inches of hope. Your new best friend. Your only chance against the enemy. Do you hear me, Samson?"

He nodded. I stepped back from the line and Sergeant Raines moved forward. He would teach them how to load.

"Most soldiers get days or weeks to drill," I added, looking down the line. "You men have minutes, and since ammunition is in short supply, only ten practice rounds."

"Ten rounds!" Samson whined. "How we supposed to learn to shoot a Rebel with only ten tries?"

"Silence!" Raines bellowed.

It was his turn now and I would leave him to it.

"Don't speak until spoken to! Don't act until ordered! Don't load your weapon until I —"

"Are these the bullets?" Samson suddenly said, disbelief widening his face as he looked at the .58 caliber conical balls in his hand. "These ain't no bigger than peas!"

A raised vein pulsed across Raines's reddening face. Jacob stepped in.

"Shush, boy!" he called down the line to Samson. "The peas are lead. When they blast out the muzzle, they move fast enough to rip a hole through your guts."

Raines took a deep breath.

"Samson, step up and load your gun!"

"Sir?"

"Load it!"

Samson unhooked the copper powder flask that dangled from his belt and fumbled to open it.

"I don't know how."

"I'll guide you. Pour the premeasured powder charge down the barrel."

Samson leaned the barrel awkwardly toward him, struggled to funnel down the powder.

"Rip a patch of cloth. Place a lead ball on it."

Samson drew a length of cloth from his pocket, ripped off a patch, opened his pouch, grabbed a ball, placed the lead and patch against the muzzle.

"Ram it home!"

Samson pulled the ramrod from the barrel, dropped it on the dirt, picked it up. The ball and patch fell to the ground. He reached down, picked them up, raised the ramrod, lowered it into the barrel, and pumped it so the ball would pack against the powder charge.

"He looks like a fool!" said a man in line.

"He won't look a fool when the Rebs are charging," Jacob shot back.

"The percussion cap!" Raines boomed.

Samson's fingers opened another pouch,

pulled out a cap, pulled back the hammer, in-
serted the cap, closed the frizzen.

"Fire!"

There was a line of tin cups on a fence post
fifty yards off.

Samson raised the gun, closed one eye,
sucked in a breath and held it.

BAM!

A tin cup blew off the post. The men in line
began to whistle.

The kickback sent Samson staggering, eyes
wide, but he saw that he'd struck his target.

"Yeehah! If massa could see me —"

"RELOAD!" Raines roared, slowly raising a
revolver to point in the air over Samson's head.

The men fell silent.

Samson smiled nervously and lowered the
gun, grabbed the barrel . . .

"Ah!"

The barrel was hot and Samson released it,
but caught it before it fell.

His fingers were shaking now. The powder
spilled. He ripped the cloth, grabbed a ball . . .

Ka-bamm!

Raines shot his revolver into the air.

Samson rammed home the patch ball, fumbled for a cap, pulled back the hammer . . .

Ka-bamm! Raines fired again.

Samson's whole body trembled now. He raised the gun and it shook like a tree branch in the wind.

BAM!

The rifle fired. Samson missed.

"RELOAD! FASTER!" Raines raged.

Samson gaped at Raines as one might gape at a madman, but he reached for the powder flask, the barrel, the patch, the ball . . .

BAM!

Ka-bamm!

Another charge released in the air over Samson's head as he loaded and fired a third time.

And missed.

"Stop," Raines ordered, suddenly calm.

Samson was panting, trembling, and sweating. He stood as still as he could, the rifle shaking at his side.

Raines let the echo of the gunshot die.

"In the heat of battle, with guns firing in your ears and men exploding next to you, a good soldier can load and fire three shots per minute, and make each of them count. Blood will spatter in your face, gentlemen. You may even take a bullet in the arm or leg. But you must fill your mind with only three words: Load. Fire. Reload. Gentlemen, load your weapons!"

I returned to headquarters and watched the remainder of the training through the window.

At the end of the drill, not one cup sat on that fence post. Indeed, the rail was fairly well destroyed. These men learned faster than any enlisted men I'd seen.

Perhaps because for Jacob and his men the stakes were somehow higher.

"Keep your powder dry!" Raines called to the men as they filed away for rations. Almost as he said this, the man in line in front of Samson lost hold of his powder flask. It rolled across the snow-dusted dirt.

Samson bent down and retrieved it, then turned toward Sergeant Raines.

"Keep your powder dry!" he repeated with a wary smile.

CHAPTER 17

Jake

The Hork-Bajir welcoming committee walked after us. The campers kept their distance, fear and wonder on their moonstruck faces.

"They don't bite," I told them. "At least, not the free Hork-Bajir. The blades are just for harvesting bark. They wouldn't hurt a fly."

Richard was the first to approach a Hork-Bajir. He stuck out his hand and said, "Greetings."

The Hork-Bajir slowly raised his hands and enclosed Richard's palm in a cage of blades. Richard flinched, but didn't move away.

"Hallloooo," the Hork-Bajir grunted, shaking Richard's hand up and down several times. Once released, Richard examined his hand. Not a scratch.

A flash of light!

"This is the greatest day of my life!" Lewis said, sticking Justin's camera back into his bag.

Without a word, I reached into the bag. Retrieved the camera. Opened it. Ripped out the film. Placed the camera back in the bag.

Lewis gulped.

"Jake!" Marco's dad jogged up to our group. "So it's true? We've got people willing to help?"

"Willing and ready," Richard replied, giving Marco's dad a hearty handshake.

"Then come with us. We're running out of time!"

The thirteen campers followed Marco's dad up the hill to where Marco's mom was waiting. I swear those two were made for wilderness living. They looked younger and happier than I'd ever seen them. Like helping stranded aliens with key concepts like organization and productivity was their destiny.

I could hardly believe what I saw at the top of the hill. A hut with torchlight had become a kind of factory.

This is how it went. The first Hork-Bajir in the assembly line grabbed a stick off a pile. Using his razor-sharp wrist blades, he stripped it of all bark and knots. Then, he tossed it to the next Hork-Bajir in line. That Hork-Bajir inspected the stake and gave it a second straightening trim. If a stick was too bowed, the Hork-Bajir tossed it into a separate pile. That pile was given to the younger Hork-Bajir for sharpening. The bent sticks became the stakes at the bottom of the pits.

The sticks that passed inspection were handed on to several older Hork-Bajir. They fastened sharpened stone arrowheads to the tips. Grooves had been carved in the tips during the stripping process so that twine could be easily tied around the arrows. A last group of Hork-Bajir carried the completed spears up to the tree platforms.

Richard, Lewis, Emily, and a mother-daughter pair of campers named Meg and Chloe were assigned duties in this assembly line. I'd never seen such willing workers.

"I've got to check the progress at the dam," I told Marco's dad. "I'll be back."

Tobias had already demorphed and was flying lookout. We were taking no chances. It seemed unlikely, but the Yeerks might stage a night attack. Might go for the element of surprise.

I morphed owl and flew to the construction site. The owl's superior night vision, and the bright moonlight, allowed me to see the progress from the air. A new layer of sticks and trees topped the original dam. The water level was at least two feet higher. Water spilled over a new section of the forest.

<Where've you been, Prince Jake?> Marco, packing mud into the cracks with his tail. <You've missed all the fun with our new friends, Mr. and Mrs. Beaver.>

I landed on the bank and began to demorph.

<They've been excellent help,> Cassie said. <At first they were afraid of us. But they seem to have realized that we're just here to help, so they've gone back to work."

"That's great," I said absently.

I had to tell them. But suddenly, I wish I didn't have to say a word.

"I, uh . . . Listen. Those campers from down the valley want to help the Hork-Bajir."

<You mean, they know?> Rachel. <Jake, are you nuts?>

"Drastic times call for drastic measures," I said evenly. "You used those words at the meeting yesterday."

"Oh. Okay, I did. Thanks for listening."

<This could be the beginning of something big,> Cassie said reluctantly. <The first volunteers.>

<Right,> Rachel said. <They'll tell others, encourage them to join the fight.>

<Exactly the problem!> Marco said angrily. <Jake, who decided it was okay to make public appearances?>

"Well, you, actually," I said. "And that's not an accusation. It's a fact. When you told your dad about us. You did what you had to do and so did I."

<That was different with my dad,> he said forcefully. <Maybe even with those sailors and marines on the aircraft carrier. I don't know. But come on, Jake. You don't even know these campers. Who they work for, who they're related to, where they're from.>

"They're a bunch of sci-fi fanatics who believed in aliens before Tobias and I even showed them anything." I tried to smile, pretend I wasn't as worried as Marco. "They thought we were from the Federation. Can you believe it?"

No one laughed.

- -

The countdown has begun.

It will all be over very, very soon.

- -

CHAPTER 18

<Prince Jake.> Ax. <Time is running out. We need your help to finish the dam.>

Not a word about what I'd done. With all that had happened between us, all that had gone down in this war, Ax still considered me his leader. Still followed my orders and accepted my decisions.

Not that it really mattered what Ax, or anyone else, thought. As long as they acted with loyalty. As long as they also understood that I'd already taken full responsibility for revealing us to the campers. Nobody else was to blame. Not even Tobias.

I focused on the newest DNA I carried inside me.

SWZOOP!

My body began to shrink. Arms and legs sucked into my torso.

FWUMP!

I hit the ground.

PING PING PING . . .

Thick brown fur sprouted all over my body. I felt suddenly warm, like I'd pulled on a wet suit.

POOT. POOT.

My back legs reappeared as short little flipper-feet.

THWUMP.

A heavy weight pulled on my rear end.

I turned my head around.

Stretching my spine almost two feet beyond my main body was a thick, flat, formidable mass. A paddle, a tool, a tail.

Morphing is unpredictable. The most dramatic changes often happen last.

Finally, my skull began to shrink, squeezing my brain into a new shape. Rock-hard skull bones, heavier than a human's, elongated to form a very rugged jaw.

And inside, my front teeth were growing. And growing.

And growing . . .

I opened and closed the jaw. Could feel the strength of the incisors, huge as carpenters' chisels, sprouting from my gums.

The beaver didn't have the raw, quick strength of a tiger. But it did have amazing stamina.

And its mind was smart in a goal-oriented, problem-solving kind of way.

The beaver felt anxious to get to its project. Its mind was alive with a single thought.

There are things to be done!

It was the mind of a workaholic.

There was a sapling. A dead branch just ahead. A vine beyond. Choose one and move!

I was an enlightened worker bee.

An ant with a college education.

I slid off the shore into the dark pond. Swam with my head above the water. The beaver's oily fur repelled the water, keeping its skin dry.

I paddled purposefully down a small canal. Away from the pond and toward the place where Ax was gnawing through a large tree.

<We need this tree for the main spillway,> he said.

I climbed out of the water and started to chew.

Oh, it felt good to sink my teeth into the tree fibers. To efficiently rip them away.

Scraping more layers with each pass! Carving through the growth rings!

Suddenly, Ax cried, <Stop! Get back!>

The tree quivered in the rising wind.

Creeeekkkkk!

The wonderful sound of splintering wood.

Ba-boom!

The tree crashed to the ground.

The beaver mind was pleased. But wait . . .

The tree wasn't aligned with the canal. It had fallen across it. Ax and I stood up on our hind legs and pushed. The tree rocked but we couldn't dislodge it.

<We need some help down here!> I shouted.

Marco and Cassie joined us. The four of us pushed together. The tree rocked up and down the sides of the impression it had made when it fell. But it still wasn't going anywhere.

The beaver was frustrated. It felt it had failed. Suddenly . . .

"Rrrrooooaaaarrr!"

In one sudden movement the tree rose off the ground! Twisted around in the air. Aligned with the canal and crashed into the water. Bobbed crazily, then calmed.

<You just need the right tool for the job.> Rachel's grizzly snorted proudly in the moonlight. <Now let's get this thing into place.>

Mr. and Mrs. Real Beaver disappeared at the sight of Rachel. But the five of us pushed and pulled at the tree, like tugboats guiding an oil tanker into the harbor.

The log moved easily into the pond and

toward the dam. Ax had shaped a place for it. We nudged it in. The current flowing over the top of the dam did the rest.

<Are you ready?> Tobias, from overhead.

<Almost,> Ax said proudly. <The water volume has exceeded my predictions.>

<It better have,> Tobias replied. <Because the Yeerks are less than an hour away. And, Jake? There are more of them than we thought.>

CHAPTER 19

Isaiah
Fitzhenry

Dusk, and still no sign of Forrest's forces. Will he wait until dawn?

Forrest has a reputation to uphold. That's hard to do in darkness. Strike at night and bravery and flamboyance go unseen.

The Negros drilled once more, then stacked their rifles and returned to the earthworks to finish the job.

When I walked down to inspect the works, I found the men singing a low, rhythmic song.

"Lieutenant," Jacob called. "My men are mighty happy with the training and the food."

"We'd have won the war a year ago with more volunteers like you." I paused. "Jacob, do you and your men wish to be mustered in?"

"Sir?"

"Sworn into service as Union soldiers. All the white men are and I thought that perhaps . . ."

"Just tell us what we need to do," he said eagerly.

The singing stopped. Heads began to turn my way.

"Just gather 'round, I suppose. I've, uh . . . I've never done this before."

I had a copy of the oath in a beat-up pamphlet found among Major Shaw's effects.

I pulled it from my pocket.

The hardworking, sweat-covered men gathered close.

"Raise your right hands, I would guess."

Thirty strong and calloused hands lifted into the air.

"Now, I'll just read the oath a line at a time. You repeat it back, see? It starts with your name, so go ahead and fill that in yourself. . . . Let's see, now . . ."

I cleared my throat and flipped to the water-soiled page entitled "Oath of Muster."

I imagined I was Lincoln. I summoned the most presidential voice I had.

"'I, Isaiah Goodhue Fitzhenry, do solemnly swear that I will bear true allegiance to the United States of America, and . . .'"

"Lieutenant?"

"Samson?"

"Can you stop there?"

"Of course."

I let the men repeat back the phrase. They filled in their own names — a sound, to me, sweet as music.

Jacob, Samson, Moses, Washington, Jackson, Jefferson, and Tennessee . . .

Thirty men to replace my own.

Tomorrow we would fight.

And stand or fall together.

I continued the oath.

"'And that I will serve them honestly and faithfully against all their enemies and opposers whatsoever . . .'"

Is General Forrest in his tent now, playing cards, sipping gin, or writing home, perhaps?

Confident that he will crush the boys in blue up on this mountain?

"'And observe and obey the orders of the President of the United States, and the orders of the officers appointed over me . . .'"

The orders we have might be the last we ever receive. May it not be so.

"'According to the rules and articles for the government of the armies of the United States.'"

The men repeated back the last phrase.

A momentary silence while I checked the page, then told them that was all.

They were soldiers.

Wild cheers erupted.

The men jumped and hollered and I lost myself in their joy.

Let their clapping hands chase away the dread.

Let their voices, which broke slowly into song, draw me home, until that's all I saw.

The crackling fire.

My sister, curled up with a book on the floor before the hearth.

Ma in her rocking chair, with her mending bag.

The smell of bread baking in the kitchen, the feel of Rover's fur on my fingers. The taste of ale.

The sound of Ma's gentle soprano humming in the corner.

I was home.

If I fall in battle, I might be home again by sundown tomorrow.

CHAPTER 20
Jake

We started to demorph. Based on their current position, the Yeerks had chosen to attack at dawn. It was showtime.

<Tobias, what did you see?>

<You know my eyes aren't great at night. But I could make out at least one company of heavily armed Hork-Bajir. More than a hundred strong. And they have blue bands around their arms.>

My heart began to pound. The Blue Bands. Visser One's own elite guards.

"Tell me that's all you saw."

<Can't lie, Jake. There are almost as many Taxxons.>

My stomach knotted.

<Oh. And one Andalite.>

Visser One. Our old nemesis, the former Visser Three. Andalite-Controller. Commander of every Yeerk on Earth. Only a mission of the highest importance draws Visser One to the scene.

"It wouldn't be a party without the Earl of Evil," Marco said solemnly.

I sent Tobias ahead to the Hork-Bajir camp. We followed, racing through the trees and down the hill. When we arrived, Tobias was announcing the news.

<The Yeerks are coming and coming strong. Everyone take up battle positions.>

Thought-speak was still new to the campers. Emily touched her hands to her head in confusion.

"No, you're not losing your mind," I said. "Morphs let us communicate telepathically. That was Tobias." I pointed up through the trees.

<Hey, I can see those campers a mile away!> Tobias said privately. <Tell them to lose the yellow coats. They're sitting ducks.>

"You people have to blend in," I said. "Bury your coats and anything else yellow or orange or fluorescent green. Then get some camouflage. Anything but earth tones will get you killed."

The campers covered their gear.

Lewis took up position on a battle platform with a Hork-Bajir warrior. A guy whose right arm had been blown off during one of the free Hork-Bajir's raids on Yeerk facilities.

The air crackled with prebattle tension. Bodies gave off the strong smells of fear and adrenaline.

Richard stared silently up at his son.

"Move anyone who's hit up behind the boulders," I shouted. "Anyone who's killed on the field, we'll have to leave until later. Until after."

Richard walked over to me, still wearing his bright yellow vest, his face clean.

"When you say 'killed,'" he asked quietly, "you mean 'killed' as in 'stunned' or 'captured,' right?"

"Unfortunately, Mr. Carpenter, I mean killed as in dead."

Richard's eyes widened, and I knew it was the first phase of panic. I'd made the dangers of this mission clear, hadn't I? Yes. This was just a guy who'd let the excitement overwhelm him. If he panicked, he could screw up everything.

"Oh, my God," he whispered, voice harsh. Like he'd thought all along that my graphic warnings were just part of some game, some dialogue from a *Deep Space Nine* episode. "I didn't realize. I've seen enough. We're going home. Lewis! Emily! Get down from there!"

I put a hand on his arm, tried to calm and silence him. "It's too late," I said. "You can't leave now."

"I'm not going anywhere!" Lewis shouted from the tree platform. "These guys need our help."

Richard shook off my hand. "Come down now or you lose all privileges for a month!" he shouted wildly.

"No, Dad." Lewis's voice was strong. "I'm staying."

<Quiet!> Tobias yelled. <They're close.>

"Battle morphs. Now!"

Richard stared at me. Paralyzed, panicked, scared. Waiting for me to save him.

I started to go tiger. "Get out of here, Richard," I told him while I still had a mouth. "Get up behind those boulders. You'll be all right. Just stay out of the way."

He glanced up at his son, then back at me. His mouth opened but nothing came out. Then he turned and ran up the hill.

The sky in the east glowed a pale and brightening blue. The sun would appear in minutes. Free Hork-Bajir were hunched in the trees and crouched low in trenches. We were in battle morph. Tiger, gorilla, grizzly, and wolf. Ax was stationed at the dam.

There wasn't a sound in the camp except a gentle rustle of wind in the treetops. We waited. My heart pounded like a rock in my chest.

This would be a losing battle. It had to be.

CHAPTER 21

Near silence. The light from the sun grew brighter. A gray mist rose off the earth.

Kwreeek!

A snapping twig.

<Quiet!> I commanded. Our defense depended upon surprise. Without it . . .

Movement!

And another sound.

Quick rhythmic footfalls striking moist earth. I searched through the mist. A glint caught my eye. A blade. Attached to a seven-foot-tall Hork-Bajir.

He paused at the edge of camp. Turned slowly, pointed his Dracon beam everywhere he looked.

More footfalls. More blades. More Hork-Bajir

with blue bands on their arms until the edge of camp overflowed with soldiers. They paused and scanned. Searching.

Then, a smaller Hork-Bajir walked toward the center of camp. It was the free Hork-Bajir captured on the raid and now infested. The Yeerk in his head had led the enemy here. It was his job to turn over the free Hork-Bajir. To betray his people.

<Steady!> I warned.

The weapons we had — spears and arrows, teeth and claws — would only work at close range. Our attack had to come at the last possible second.

<On my word . . .>

The Blue Bands began to move forward. In seconds they would fall into our camouflaged trenches. In moments, they would be close enough to touch.

The newly infested Hork-Bajir brought something that looked like a cell phone to his mouth.

"All gone, Visser."

Unbelievable. He'd reported we weren't there! Maybe the soldiers would give up, turn away, retreat . . .

But then he raised his eyes into the trees, and froze. We'd been spotted.

<ATTACK!>

Pthoo! Pthoo! Thoo, thoo, thoo, thoo!

A rain of heavy spears, arrows, and sharp rocks pelted the enemy before they could fire.

"GhaaaaaLhaaaa!"

Cassie bounded across the dirt. Clamped her wolf jaws around a Hork-Bajir ankle.

<Ah!>

A gash bloodied her flank. She didn't let go.

<Heeyahhh!>

Marco, a hulking gorilla charging into the advancing line of Blue Bands.

Whoompf! Whoompf!

His wrecking-ball fists slammed two warriors to the ground.

Thwoosh! Thwoosh, thoosh, thoosh!

Toby slashed into the fray, nimbly slicing the enemy with wrist, knee, and ankle blades. Skillfully anticipating strikes before they came.

The free Hork-Bajir screamed. Jumped from tree platforms onto the backs of the enemy. Drove their ankle blades deep into the backs of the Blue Bands.

ZING ZING ZING!

The sound of blades whipping through the air as Hork-Bajir battled Hork-Bajir in a sad civil war.

I lunged. Gripped the small Hork-Bajir in my jaw. Dragged him back behind our line. Two free Hork-Bajir were waiting with restraints. They would bring him to Marco's parents, tending the wounded. They'd hold him. Hide him. Hope that, in the end, they could starve the Yeerk from his head.

I raced back to the battle.

Sprang at the biggest Blue Band I could find. Sank my fangs into the back of his neck. Felt his muscles slacken, watched him fall.

Tseeew!

The air over my head crackled with the sound of Dracon fire, flashing blue and white like lightning.

I lunged for another Blue Band.

Bam!

Slammed him against the trunk of a tree.

Thumph!

We crashed to the dirt and rolled.

Knocked into fallen Hork-Bajir. Bodies were beginning to cover the floor of the valley. Those with blue bands and those without.

Rachel's grizzly galloped into view. Charged a Hork-Bajir pointing a Dracon beam into the trees.

Wooomph!

Tseeew!

Bam!

She clobbered him, drove him into a rock. But he'd discharged his weapon. The tree burst into flames. A battle platform incinerated!

Agonizing cries, . . .

Another flood of arrows and spears pounded the ground. Bounced harmlessly off blades. Sank lethally into flesh.

"Ghaaaaaah!"

The air was thick with this deadly rain. Lewis and Emily. Meg and Chloe. The other campers and Hork-Bajir. Heaving spear after spear.

And the Blue Bands ducked and ran . . . back the way they had come.

Retreat?

A moment of stunned silence. Then, the free Hork-Bajir began to shout. To jump up and down. To dance.

Those on the ground emerged from the battle trenches. Cries of triumph filled the air. Warriors shook their spears above their heads. Even the campers began to smile. The few captured Dracon beams were fired into the air.

I knew better. Marco, the others. We weren't celebrating.

The victory dance was premature.

I'd just spotted him, through the trees and mist, silently approaching as the Hork-Bajir and campers cheered.

Visser One. In a morph I hadn't seen since all of this first began. Eight fire-breathing heads. Legs thick as trees. Serpentine necks. Eyes like gobs of molten lava.

I staggered back.

Because behind the mammoth, monstrous visser came an undulating line of Taxxons. A lumbering line of death.

<Positions!> I screamed above the naive yells of victory. <Stop! Look! They're coming again!>

The joyous voices fell silent. Laughter tumbled into desperate, flustered cries as warriors rushed to ready their weapons. To draw fresh sticks and spears from piles.

And then came the voice. That crackling, roaring, crushing voice.

<You are outnumbered! Surrender at once. Or die!>

CHAPTER 22

Isaiah
Fitzhenry

Christmas morning.

A shrill bugle call startled me from sleep. There was a pounding on the door of headquarters where I slept, fully dressed, in the corner.

I jumped to my feet, grabbed my long gun and revolver, and opened the door.

"They're here," Raines said, eyes wide, face calm. "A small force in the trees, same as yesterday."

We threw our guns on our shoulders and ran.

The bugle stopped and, for a moment, the only sound was the pounding of boots on the dirt as Union men converged on the works. Rifles rattled as they ran. Flasks and canteens knocked together.

Spears was already there, loading the one artillery piece we'd managed to tow with us.

"Looks like a frontal attack, Lieutenant," he gasped as he and Price released the massive ball into the barrel.

I raised my field glass and focused on the Rebel line formed in the trees. My heart began to hammer. I could see the panting horse noses, the gray flannel coats, the shining saber sheaths.

Why weren't there more than yesterday?

Could the Rebel prisoner have been wrong? Could the force not number more than the hundred troopers Spears had seen?

"Lieutenant!"

I turned toward town. A group of ten men loped toward our line, shotguns and pitchforks in tow. Joe Miller waved.

"This is our town and, by God, we'll fight to keep it."

It was nearly all the men from Sinkler's Ridge. Even the drummer boy and penny whistler had revolvers in their hands.

My smile was faint but genuine. "It's good to see you, Joe. It's a frontal attack. Would you serve as flankers?"

Joe directed five men to the east end of the line and took the rest with him to the west.

"TAKE AIM!" I ordered.

The Rebels edged out from the trees. Why didn't they charge? What were they waiting for?

I raised my field glass again, ran it down the Rebel line, and picked out a face among the branches. A thin man, with dark hair and prominent cheekbones that stretched his skin almost violently. Stars dotted his collar. The horse beneath him was the only equine not chafing at the bit. Shadows concealed the man's eyes. Strung across his chest was not one carbine, but two.

Was it Forrest?

Why didn't he charge? Why?

"Raines? Spears? Are you ready?"

"Yes, sir, Lieutenant!"

"Jacob?"

"Ready, sir."

Would this be the day that Forrest fell?

Joe Miller crouched behind the works, steadying his aim against the piled dirt.

We were ready. Yet I felt that something . . . something was wrong. . . .

"CHARGE!"

The Rebel troopers pulled out from the woods, whooping, hollering, galloping over and around slashed trees.

"TAKE AIM!" I repeated nervously.

The Rebs raised their guns.

"SPEARS, FIRE!"

BA-BAMMM!

The cannon whistled.

Ka-boom!

"Ahhh!"

Two horses and troopers were thrown into the air.

"FIRE!"

BAMM! BAMM!

For one instant, pride swelled my heaving chest. This was the largest force I had ever commanded. . . .

"FIRE!" the Rebel commander yelled.

Lead shot cut the frozen air. An indiscriminate wave of death.

"Yahhh!"

"Ahh!"

"Ah-ahhhh!"

Men were falling, crying, screaming.

Samson was down. And Spears.

"STEADY, MEN! RELOAD!"

I heard the wild rattle of ramrod and hammer.

"FIRE!"

We shot again. The Rebels galloped on.

Screams and cries met my ears as we brought the enemy to the ground.

"RELOAD!"

"FIRE!"

The Rebels wavered, drawing back short of our trenches.

All at once it began to rain. Icy drops splattered my face.

"They're retreating!" Raines yelled.

Was it possible?

Forrest would sooner die than take defeat.

No. Something in this was wrong.

All wrong.

CHAPTER 23

The rain came in a torrent now, turning the works to mud.

The Rebel line broke and scattered back toward the trees.

It couldn't be victory.

Jacob poured a powder charge and ripped a patch from his shirt.

"Jacob," I called. "You've done your fighting. You've shown you can stand with the white men and not fail. Now go! Escape to the hills!"

Jacob continued loading.

Men all around us, black and white, were moaning.

All were bloody. Some were motionless.

The men who'd been spared did what they could.

Tied makeshift bandages around the wounds.

Offered drinks from canteens.

"Listen to me, Jacob! Forrest will be back. He'll make prisoners of us, but he will kill you. Do you hear me? Save your men, Jacob. It's your duty as a leader."

Jacob looked up now. I'd gotten through.

"I want all you men who still can to choose life. Get back up into them hills and stay alive to fight another day."

No one moved.

"Move out!" he cried, shaking his arm.

Still, no one moved.

Suddenly, a drum beat from the east.

We froze. Me, Jacob, everyone.

Another drum beat from the west.

To our east and west was nothing but craggy rock, terrain impossible to climb on horseback.

"We'll be staying," Jacob said.

"You'll die."

"Lieutenant, the Lord may take me whenever he chooses. But I choose whether to die a free man fighting for what's mine, or a coward enslaved by fear."

The Rebel yell rose like the cries of a thousand demons.

Through the curtain of rain, I watched horse

after horse strain and struggle up and over the rocky pass.

"They're attacking on the west!" Miller yelled from the other end of our line.

"And the south!" Raines shouted. "They're riding up from the south again!"

"TAKE AIM!"

The mud sucked at my boots, the rain pounded my back.

"Aim where?" Raines yelled.

"At the closest target!"

The men raised their rifles.

Townsmen raised their shotguns.

Our line stood firm as Rebs galloped at us from three sides, powering through the rising fog.

"FIRE!" I yelled.

Our lead blasted east, west, south.

There were cries from the enemy. We'd shot well. They were falling!

But not enough.

From the east alone, no less than a hundred troopers poured from the gap in the rock.

"RELOAD!"

The motion was almost futile in the rain. Water poured down our barrels, soaking the powder.

"FIRE!" the Rebel leaders cried.

Suddenly, time stopped.

I fired my revolver at the swarming mass of animals and men.

They were closing in on our melting fortifications . . .

Closing in . . .

WHAM!

The impact threw me to the mud.

My chest!

I reached for it. No need to open my coat. The blood was there. Already on the surface.

Just under my heart.

Flowing through my fingers.

Gushing down my ribs.

"No," I breathed.

I turned my head, looking for hope.

For help . . .

The Rebs had broken our line to the west. . . .

I can see Jacob fighting. Swinging his musket like a club, like he swung his shovel on the first day.

Striking the troopers streaming though.

No, behind you! Jacob!

Bamm!

Jacob. Shot in the back.

His eyes catch mine . . .

As he falls . . .

And I fall . . .

Together.

CHAPTER 24

Jake

The retreating Hork-Bajir-Controllers stopped just beyond the range of our spears. Turned. Aimed their Dracon beams at the trees and picked off one free Hork-Bajir at a time.

Free Hork-Bajir screamed. Scrambled down from the platforms. Flames devoured tree after tree. Along with the brave warriors who didn't make it in time.

Then . . .

"Ssssssny-ssssnit-ssssnit-sssnnnaaaaaa!"

Taxxons poured through camp.

"Skreeeeeeeeeeeeeee!"

The first tumbled into the pits, impaled by the wooden spears. The skewered bodies, two and three layers deep, made a bridge for those who followed. The Taxxons surged toward the fallen Hork-Bajir. Some stopped to feast on their own dead. Some didn't.

"Rrrrrrrrroaaaagh!"

I leaped. Sank my teeth into slippery, puffy skin. Disgusting. Like piercing a balloon filled with something hot and foul.

I stumbled away from the deflated body.

Saw Rachel squeeze a Taxxon until it burst.

Heard Cassie snarling frantically. Marco bellowing.

<Tobias!> No answer. I broadcast my thought-speak as loud as I knew how. <The water! Tell Ax. NOW!>

Hork-Bajir elders and youth ran chaotically. Crying, howling. The forest burned around them. Sniper fire sprayed the trees, the ground.

Everywhere, the free Hork-Bajir were falling. Dying.

<Out of the camp!> I yelled. <Everyone get into the hills. The water's coming!>

But how could I be sure? Why hadn't Tobias answered? Was he down? Would Ax get the message?

A Taxxon reared up behind me. I leaped into a turn. Sank my fangs into its miserable, bloated mass.

The battle was a mess and I was responsible.

I turned and raced up the valley, toward the

dam that Ax would open with his tail blade. If he ever got the order.

Suddenly . . .

ZWIIIP! ZWIIIP!

Streaks of blinding orange stuff raced through the air. Flying fireballs.

Visser One!

I froze.

Eight colossal legs, thick as trunks, stormed through the woods. The ground shook! Full-grown trees snapped like toothpicks.

Eight horrific heads with simmering orange eyes belched balls of flame.

Then . . .

"Tseeer!"

<Tobias! No!>

Tobias, diving at the monster again and again. Scratching eyeballs with his talons. Ripping flesh with his beak.

But he was no more than a flea to the visser's giant monster, inflicting more annoyance than pain. The monster's eight spindly arms clutched at the air. Unless Tobias flew to safety, the tentacles were going to catch him!

<Tobias, stop! That's an order!>

I felt my throat closing. My mouth clenched with fear. I sent another desperate thought-speak message to Ax. Prayed he would hear.

<Open the dam! Send the water! NOW!>

A horrible screech!

Tobias was hit! Slapped off by a tentacle. Hurled into the trees!

The visser's monster morph stomped closer to the fleeing Hork-Bajir. Fireball after fireball flew from its mouths. Young and old alike, instantly incinerated.

No choice. I charged. Bounded over the fallen bodies of sagging Taxxons and burnt Hork-Bajir. And in one gigantic leap of pure power, all my strength and speed concentrated in one blow . . .

I smashed into the visser. Sank my four-inch fangs into one of the monster's eight serpentine necks.

<You're pitiful,> he growled. <You will die.>

I bit harder, jaw tightening like a vice. Extended the claws on all four paws so they pierced the bleeding neck.

Barely hung on as the neck whipped the tiger through the air like a rag.

The monster's red-hot blood burned my mouth.

But as long as I held on, the visser couldn't fire at me. If he did, he'd burn himself.

He could, however, strike at me with the teeth of neighboring heads. Teeth that glowed hot as branding irons.

Tssssss!

<Ahhh!>

I twisted and dodged, dug deeper with my claws. Barely enough strength to hold on!

Tsssssssssss!

Hot teeth burned a hole in my back! Flesh scalded! Muscle seared! It was agony!

WWUMPH?

I lost my grip. Fell to the ground. Rolled onto the bank of the stream.

I struggled to get up, but a tremendous weight pushed me back down. Crushed me so I could barely breathe.

<At last,> the visser roared. Two of eight clawed hands closed around my neck. Three of eight heads breathed scalding breath into my face.

And I knew I was dead.

CHAPTER 25

Thoooph! Thoooph! Thoooph!

Fireballs shot from his mouth!

I shut my eyes and screamed.

<Ahhhhhhhhh!>

Then . . .

A cool, tingling sensation from the tiger's head to tail.

And I was tumbling. Swept mindlessly away by a forceful current.

Body spinning, out of control . . .

Was this death by fire? Strange. Was this the end?

<Aaaaaarrgh!>

Visser One's voice, raging in my ear. What?

I opened my eyes. Not flames. Water!

The opened dam!

And then I saw the visser's monster swept off its feet.

Eight ludicrous legs waved in the air.

Eight long necks, whipped by the current into knots.

The monster's fire was squelched.

<Ahhhhhh!>

His roar filled the valley, the forest.

I had to save myself!

Coughing. Choking. Drowning.

The world rushing past like super-fast-speed film.

Couldn't get a grip, couldn't slow down!

The tiger spun and whirled. Gulping water, sipping air.

The visser's monster was traveling downstream with me. Tentacle-like arms smacked me. Serpentine necks slapped.

He'd entangle me again if he could. Pull me down!

Even if we both drowned in the process.

Get to the bank, Jake!

Hork-Bajir tumbled in the water all around me. Blades grazed the tiger's stomach and back.

It was a waterslide to hell.

Then I saw . . . Coughed. Gasped. No!

I was headed toward a massive tree trunk! But maybe . . .

<Yaaaah!>

I stretched out my front legs. Gripped the trunk with extended claws.

Had to hold on! But I was slipping!

The current dragged my body forward.

Had to find a way to use my back legs and claws, too.

Hug the tree for life.

WHAP!

One of Visser One's tentacle arms smashed the tree just over my head. The arm fell away, limp.

And the monster swept past me, fires extinguished, voice raging.

Still I hung on. Back throbbing, mouth numb.

Slowly . . .

The force of the current began to lessen.

The water level dropped until, finally, finally I could let go of my desperate grip.

Found myself standing in mud.

I dragged my body into the camp, splashing through mud and water and blood.

Fallen Hork-Bajir lay everywhere.

Drowned Taxxons sprawled like popped balloons.

Yeerk slugs slithered from their fallen hosts.

I spotted Rachel, still in grizzly morph, climbing to her feet in the mud.

Out from under her massive legs crawled the youngest free Hork-Bajir.

Jara Hamee and Ket Helpek's newest child. Rachel had kept him alive.

<Jake!> Cassie and Marco limped toward me.

One of her legs was bleeding badly. The skin on his chest was raw and burned.

We demorphed.

"Ax did it," I said quietly, human again. "We did it."

But it didn't feel like victory.

How could it, with so many bodies from both sides lying lifeless?

I spotted Lewis and Emily, struggling to their feet.

A few of the other campers, holding each other tight.

<Jake!>

I looked up. A hawk circled overhead.

"Tobias! You're alive!"

<Yeah. I morphed. Ax is okay, too. But Jake? There are a lot who didn't make it. Mr. Carpenter, Jake. Richard. Emily and Lewis lost their dad.>

CHAPTER 26

The aftermath of battle.

I heard sobbing up on the hill. Emily sat with her hands covering her face. Lewis stared at his sister, blank-faced and lost.

Tobias and Cassie had broken the news.

I wouldn't have known what to say.

Toby had a diagonal slash across her chest and blood dripping from her fingers, but she was seeing to her people.

Comforting, commending.

Explaining that it was time to leave the valley.

At least for a while.

Marco's parents acted as the primary medics, tying tourniquets and organizing the uninjured to help the wounded.

Those warriors too hurt to walk were dragged in stretchers made of branches, bark, and rope.

Everyone mourned the dead, but the colony knew it had to move out quickly.

Now that the trees had burned, Visser One might be back with Bug fighters. He might be mad enough to risk detection.

It would be a long and painful march up and out of the valley and into the hills.

I pulled Toby away from her preparations.

"You know they'll be back. Not today, but soon."

She nodded.

"I know, Jake. But we won today. It may not feel like victory, but the valley is ours now. Forever. We've paid for it."

She took a deep breath.

"We'll stay away until the war is over. We know we have to. We had our chance to fight for freedom. That's all we really wanted."

"Toby," I said softly, "I don't know how the war will end."

"No. But it will. And someday . . ." She hesitated.

She knew as well as I that if the Yeerks won out, she and the other free Hork-Bajir would be enslaved.

I finished her thought for her.

"Someday," I said, "you'll be able to return."

She looked at me, eyes full of hope.

After the free Hork-Bajir headed out of the valley, Marco and his parents leading the way, I flew to Cassie's farm.

Demorphed and walked home in the early afternoon sun.

Tobias had promised that by the time I got to my house, the Chee covering for me would be gone. Just.

My parents — and Tom — would know nothing.

I was shaking and weak by the time I reached the front door. Yes, I was hungry and tired, but it was more than that.

I slipped quietly in through the front door. Mom, Dad, and Tom were in the backyard, hanging by the grill.

I headed for the basement. It was dark and quiet.

I felt safe there, among the boxes of accumulated memories.

Memories of times and battles past.

I flipped to the last page of Fitzhenry's journal.

"Hooves trampling the dirt all around . . . screams and wails of bloody, dying men . . . unending nightmare. Cannot get a full breath . . . numbness spreading down my arm. Vision blurring . . . growing narrow like a field glass, a darkening tunnel. . . ."

"Jake, honey? Lunch is ready."

I jumped. Mom's voice had startled me.

"Coming, Mom," I called. "I'll be right there."

"You'd better, Midget," Tom yelled down the stairs. "Or I'll eat your burger."

I looked at the diary's last words, where blood and rain had smeared the ink.

"I fear I am killed. I hope I have done my best. I hope . . ."

Those were the last legible words.

Fitzhenry had tried and lost.

How would my last page read?

How would my story end?

"I hope I have done my best."

"Yeah," I whispered, closing the book. "Me, too."

Footsteps.

I jumped, startled.

Clanging footsteps above me.

I rolled my eyes back toward the top of the cube.

A vaulted ceiling soared maybe thirty feet overhead.

At the top was a small manhole cover.

And leading from the cover was a rusted iron staircase that snaked down the far wall like a fire escape.

Once for the sewer workers.

Now for whatever lunatic had constructed this macabre den.

The two guys clanging down the staircase definitely did not work for the utility company.

They reached the bottom. Brushed the hanging cobwebs aside like they were parting a curtain. And approached my cube.

Two guys. Late teens.

Neither looked bright enough to be the mastermind behind this nightmare scenario. *Definitely not the brains of the operation, Rachel.*

One was tall and skinny. He wore dirty, torn jeans and a black T-shirt. There was a tattoo of a rat on his right cheek.

The other one was short and fat. He also wore dirty, torn jeans. But his T-shirt screamed "the Grateful Dead" in psychedelic swirls and acid-hot colors. Over that he wore a light blue windbreaker. His hair was pulled into a thin, greasy ponytail.

There is just no accounting for taste.

These guys were nothing. I could take punks like these.

These guys looked like they survived on a diet of Twinkies and 7UP.

They were mine.

I'd say nothing.

I'd wait for them to tell me what was going on.

What they wanted.

Who they were working for.

What they'd done with Cassie.

And then I'd make them sorry they'd ever messed with me.

Tattoo looked at Grease.

"Here it is, man. Just like he said."

Grease looked around, nodded.

"Yeah, dude. This is the place. So I guess now's the time. Now is definitely the time. I guess."

Neither of the punks looked at me. Not in the face, anyway.

This was so not their deal.

Then, whose? Whose!

Stay calm, Rachel. Stay calm.

Assess before you act.

Don't do anything stupid.

Grease reached into his jacket pocket. I saw now that it was bulging.

Slowly, carefully he produced . . .

A rat.

Of course. Of course.

Dreams of rats, rats in the walls, rats in the basement, rats in my shirt . . .

If you weren't such a harsh person, Rachel . . .

Gently, Grease put the rat down on the table or platform. Placed it right in front of me, just on the other side of the clear wall of the cube.

We were inches apart, me and the rat.

It was large.

A rat that gazed up at me with a stange intelligence in its little beady eyes.

A rat that looked at me as if it knew something important about me.

As if it recognized me.

I'll kill you! I'll kill you! I'll kill you!

One of its own . . .

If you weren't such a harsh person . . .

Of course. Of course.

<Hello, Rachel,> said the rat. <Did you miss me?>

I wasn't surprised.

I wasn't scared, either.

This was a dream. Just another dream.

I'd wakened from the others. I'd wake from this one, too.

"David," I said, feeling more curious than anything else.

I was smarter than any of you . . .

<Surprised?>

"No," I answered truthfully.

I shifted, tried to find some way to be comfortable inside the cube. My right foot was falling asleep. My lower back was beginning to ache.

It was time to wake up.

<Scared?> the rat named David asked.

I was smarter . . .

"No," I answered, truthful again.

You can't judge me!

And then the rat chuckled.

<Oh, well, it's still early. And no, Rachel, this isn't a dream. You're not going to wake up. Not this time.>

ANIMORPHS®

K. A. Applegate

Also available:

Available wherever you buy books, or use this order form.

Scholastic Inc., P.O. Box 7502, Jefferson City, MO 65102

Please send me the books I have checked above. I am enclosing $_____ (please add $2.00 to cover shipping and handling). Send check or money order–no cash or C.O.D.s please.

Name_____ Birth date_____

Address_____

City_____ State/Zip_____

Please allow four to six weeks for delivery. Offer good in U.S.A. only. Sorry, mail orders are not available to residents of Canada. Prices subject to change. ANIB1100

http://www.scholastic.com/animorphs